The Dead Bod Man
By Asa Montreaux

Apollo Books Press

Apollo Books Press ©
Asa Montreaux ©

Apollo Books Press

Vancouver, BC
Canada

Originally Published June 13, 2024

The Dead Bod Man   Apollo Books

1

Apollo Books

One

-

How many more years before I make a difference in this city. Sometimes I feel there is something terrible, but no one knows. It is not so much a tradeoff, but a fact of reality. In fact, we don't mention it. Sure, you can read about it in the paper. But you aren't here… you just don't experience it. The dirty, disgusting, murders of the city of New York.

You don't need to believe what I am saying, you only need to read about it. And believe me. It won't be anything you had expected it to be.

Two

-

We got a call to head out and me and my partner

hopped in the car to get to the scene. I am a detective

on the NYPD. I'm a lead detective. My name is

Bernardo Soulaz. My partner is Edmund Chow, also a

detective on the NYPD.

You think you've seen it all. But this mother fuckin'

night. We saw the worst we had ever seen. At least

up to that point.

We had the siren on half the trip. Traffic had blocked

up half the avenues, and we had to beat it to get the

evidence before the news trucks came around.

As I stepped out of the police cruiser, the yellow tape

began right in front of us. A man, face down, with a

bullet in the back of his head. And a significant

amount of his guts were splattered around him. He had fallen from the eleventh story. We walked in the building. Sitting at the reception was a woman. Her head was laying across a register. She was dead as well, with a bullet right between her eyes.

2

One

-

Do you always wait for the longest day of the year and then miss it. I bet you fucking do. There was never anything stupider and more animal like than a sexy woman. Oh my god I just want to come in the face of anything with double dees and decent looks. In fact I am not sure I can write this I so have the urge to fucking blow one off thinking about anal fucking a sex goddess and then dumping poopy cum all of her eyes and nose and mouth. Sometimes after I beat them to death with my dick. Right after. I thought I'd do it unreal life a lot of time. There always fucking dead by the time I'm done though.

Two

-

I didn't care who I killed. I just killed them. It was like being the wind, I just blew, and whoever was in the way, they were blown. I'd stand outside the Cabaret, our outside Mario's, and whenever they wanted the pills, they'd come grab them for three, four hundred bucks every time. It was almost every time I killed them. There was enough of the lethal mix inside each one to kill anyone. I sat there deciding whether to make the good ones, or the, you know, lethal ones, and nearly every time, I decided to make the lethal ones. All I could see is that would give me the most pleasures. Just to see those fuckers just rot the fuck away. They'd never know it was me. They were tricked. Hah. And in an instant I had taken away their precious life, making them the brainless automatons they were, and for always.

As I sat there making the pills, I knew there was something missing for me in it. It didn't give me the fulfillment I had wanted. It wasn't like when I killed a woman I had been stalking. I could convince them eh date me, and within a few fucks I fucking slaughtered *every one of those cunts. There was nothing better than being the eye of their desire when they could not figure out you were anything but someone who should be that. When they couldn't see it was all a trick, and that they were only chosen to ultimately satisfy me, and give me all the pleasure int eh world by seeing their blood fly across the fucking room, and smear all of the fucking walls. I masturbated so hard cleaning blood of the walls of those hotel rooms it was almost better than the kill itself. I'd grab their dead bodies and fuck their mouths so hard they'd fucking bleed while they were dead. And then my fucking blood out my dick was fucking intermingling with their dead mouth cock blood and they were my*

fucking victims for life in the most sacred way ever

fathomable.

Thinking about this I had to masturbate right way. It

was the most uncontrollable urge. And I had to bleed,

I squeezed and tugged so hard, that my dick nearly

burst it started bleeding spots hard. And even after I

came, the semen all stained red and orange from the

blood, even after it land on the pictures of my new

stupid victims and after I emptied the remains right on

their faces int he pictures, I was still beating it, for

fucking twenty minutes, until I eventually the pain

passed and I came another three times, right in their

fucking faces, until the point where I needed so bad

to go kill them right then, I almost screwed up my

whole plan. But in the end, that got me too hard, and I

blew off one last one, my dick shriveled at that point,

working over time, so that I knew the ultimate would

be pulling off my plan.

Three

-

So who would go first among the three of them. Who

could say? If I was someone else I might say that.

There was one woman. And two men. No one knew

Sometimes I get a bat and smash their heads up while I fuck their mouths. Until there's nothing left of the jaw. At that point I'm finished. And then I just have to clean it up.

The trouble was with the first one. The writer boy. There were too many people that knew him around town. Taking out someone famous was tough to do. I think that's what it was with this one. It was the difficulty of it. When the gratification of completing the job came, I knew it was going to be so great, so transcendent, there wasn't going to be any kills in the past that were as good. These were going to be the most meaningful ones of my life. And I was only looking forward to it.

And then there was the business ace. The ceo, no, the doesn't c he's not going to be alive soon. He was the youngest managing partner in town. Leading the firm to huge profits. All of New York raved about him. He had his fame too. All the kills this one were not easy. I wasn't going to forget to mention it. But he's writer boy's lawyer. Take him out and you're home free.

They're all a little famous. And then there is writer boy's girlfriend. The struggling model. The prettiest woman I have ever seen. Twenty's, huge breasts, the most gorgeous photos you've ever seen. But not the right connections. It was time to end it before it became a real career. It would be only me that knew, that she was the hottest chick alive. And I would be the one that had her. The last one to have her. And the only one to really have her. The only one to have her while her skin is all gone, and the only things left are her vagina and her fucking mouth. I am going to miss having this one. It will be the best one and only having the memory will honestly be a little sadder.

3

One
-

Being the greatest lawyer in town was not only the privilege of a lifetime, but the very symbol of pride that the whole family of Geesonn's cherished like the Holy Trinity. It meant everything to them that Salazar had become the greatest Lawyer around.

The odd fact of the matter is that he was young, and not many articles had been written about him. It was not very well known amongst the public that there was never a better arguer, or a lawyer with a better trial record. But at the same times, word moves swiftly from clients to their business partners, so that Salazar was quickly becoming the most in demand lawyer in the city. And someone recognized in a lot of circles as exactly what he was, the greatest lawyer of all time.

It was time for the most discomforting conversation of his career, and also of his life. The matter affected his life deeply. And the call was with his favorite client, and the most likeable client he had ever had, and surely that anyone had ever had. There was nothing that had changed with the client. He was still the most likeable person on the planet. Though the matters surrounding his life had the air of graveness about them to smite popularity. You wouldn't be laughing after you heard it, all of it. All of what they had so far. He'd still like his client after this phone call, though he would never just think everything is okay and perfectly fine after speaking with him again. Well, it was not, or it was never.

He picked up the phone and dialed his client's

number.

"Holden, are you okay?"

"Yes. Of course. I am okay?"

"But, is someone stalking you?"

"Yes. There is someone stalking me intensely. But…"

"What?"

"He's good, really good."

"I know. But listen, we are onto him. We have already got him."

"Had you Id'd him?"

"No. You wouldn't believe it, but he's clean. But look, that was one hell of a lead."

"Yea. There is no way this guy knows I noticed. I am sure he has never stalked someone perceptive."

"Holden. I need to know. Is he masturbating?"

The line was quite for a moment.

"Yes. He definitely was. He was doing it very loudly and moaning."

"But you're a guy. He's gay?"

"Well, there's something else."

"I am aware. I certainly hadn't forgotten. When you and your girlfriend…?"

"Yes, while we're having sex. He was masturbating very loudly."

"Do you have evidence she is a target as well."

"No, but he seemed to fixate on her."

"But he's been stalking you half the day?"

There was no answer for a second.

"Well, he probably will start stalking her if he hasn't

already."

"I agree. And there is something else. He is stalking me as well."

"Yes, how is your situation Salazar?"

"I have bodyguards, and the person hasn't been in the building. They said they could see him, and see him masturbating."

"Did they notice anything else? Anything useful?"

"He's very good at getting in and out of buildings. It's going to be a real issue. But look, I think we'll be okay. We can catch this guy. He has obviously never been caught before, but he doesn't know what he's up against, does he?"

"There is no way he does. I am sure he has no clue I even noticed. They probably would assume they are not going to be noticed until the end."

"Absolutely. That is right. That is definitely right. Okay, stay safe, alright. I will talk to you tomorrow. We are hopeful we will have more useful information."

"Okay. Talk then."

"Bye."

"Bye."

Two

-

What do all of my victims have in common?

They were fucked three hundred times at least. Some

of them the thousand.'

In fact, it was ten thousand alive, ten thousand dead.

What do they always say, oh, pretty please, don't kill

me. Sure, at first I hadn't.

But in the end, I always fucking had!!!!!!

So all of you die!!!!!

And to this lonely fucking red light looking fucker in

the park where I am. Yea, that's right I'm on the

prowl. To her, fucking die. There, I slashed her

fucking throat.

She thinks she's dying, but I'll have her alive for

another fucking number of weeks.

I'll stop that bleeding right when she's on death door.

But right now, my dick is already in her fucking

mouth. Oh fuck yea!!!!!!!

Three

-

Fionae knew the way to start the day was by jumping
out of bed, but lately she was suffering from deep
exhaustion. When she awoke, she only thought of the

sweet death of the mind of sleep. It is a million times in life we die and awake again. So she felt when she was tired, and didn't want to start her day. She knew she needed to do so after a while, she climbed out of bed, and dressed in her gown. She'd been sleeping in the nude ever since Holden left. She was suddenly reminded of it, when her boyfriend took her on the stove, before he took her in the bed, while she lay on her stomach. Before walking out of the bedroom, she bent over, and masturbated as hard as she could. She felt tired, and she nearly hurt herself and liked it so much she went harder. She imagined her boyfriend inside her and bent over further. That's what they would do next time. He'd been in her ass while she stood right her. She came in her undies, and quickly changed them, before heading to the bathroom. She couldn't find her brush at first, and strangely, she found it back in her room. She couldn't remember leaving it in there, but strange things can happen. It was surely nothing.

She ate cereal while she looked through some articles on her phone, and waited for text messages from friends, or from her agent. She wasn't expecting to hear from Holden, but then again, they always talked.

'You alright?' He asked.

'Of course. Why?' She wrote.

'Oh, no reason. So everything's fine. You got to bed okay and whatever?'

'Yes.' She related with reticence, not wanting to talk about how tired she'd been feeling, especially in the morning.

'Alright,' he wrote. 'Are you alright? You seemed just slightly not yourself a couple times yesterday.'

'You asked yesterday. I'm, okay.'

'Alright. Talk Later xo'

'Luv xoxo'

She had to be to work in a couple hours. For a model she got ready awfully quick, but she thought she better go shower anyways.

4

One

-

What a cum dumpster. Oh my fucking fucking Mary

licking god. Of fucking fucking fuck yeah. Oh fuck

yea. And meanwhile I am not hiding in one. I am right

outside her fucking window. She can't see because

she's not looking. But it she looked she see me. She

wouldn't see me beating of so fucking hard, but I am

right below the sight of the window. She's just getting

up. She's tired because I have been making so much

noise. Moaning, and jerking so hard, the entire time

she sleeps. I even talked to her while she is sleeping.

She didn't know it, but she'd been moaning half the

time she slept. It wasn't really sexual but all the

fucking better, it's like we were just fucking talking.

Fuck yea. Agghhhh.

Hopefully no one checks these fucking walls. I'll have

to just scrape them. Otherwise someone will notice all

of this. Reminder for later I guess. Right now I can't

take my eyes off her.

She's bending over. Oh my God the hand is

assuming the posish. Oh she's rammin' it. Ohhhh

Fuckkk yeaaaaa!!! Oh! Oh! Oh she's imagining it in the ass. Ahhhh! Fuck I'm moaning while she's awake. She hadn't noticed. Ah I got to go harder. More, more, more, more, more. Ah, tighter, tighter. Fuck yea, I'm bleeding. Fuck yea. Ohh my god! Oh she's still going at it. What a fucking ass. Oh my god. When she dies I am just going to destroy that shit like mother fucking Scream. Oh my GOD I cannot wait. Here comes one. Oh she's just doing a quick one, we're gonna come together and she won't even know it. Here it comes, here it comes.

Oh she's tensing up. All you have, give it all you have. Ah, Ahhhhh! Here it comes, it gonna be fucking fucking bloody! Arghhhhhhh!!!! Ah! Open you eyes, ahh she's coming too, she's coming too. Ahh get some more, get some more!!! Arghhhhhhhhhhhhhhh! Oh fuck yea!!!!! Well I get the better of this one as well. Add her to the list. She's coming with me and she doesn't know it. And one day she'll be doing it with me right in front of her and all inside of her. They always fall for every fucking trick.

Two

-

Holden couldn't believe she didn't know what was going on. He was sure if she had thought about it. She would have heard the guy. It was what Salazar had said. Half the day he's stalking you... half the day...

The other half, he was stalking her. That must be true. Otherwise what was he doing? Surely just stalking someone else. It was best not to mention it. Let her not feel scared. But he figured there would be a time to tell her, or else she wouldn't be ready for the attack. There would be a time when they couldn't be apart, when he would have to protect her every second. Maybe he could hire someone. Maybe it wasn't a good idea. Salazar didn't really need to know. Holden could hardly pay him sometimes, but if he saved enough, he could maybe afford a good bodyguard. But someone would need to be with her even in the night. It would have to be someone she trusts. That left only him.

He was ashamed of himself for a second, because he thought there might be a good novel out of this. It was an interesting story, for sure, lover boy, defending his one true love, from an evil murderer. An evil, murderer, stalker. And there he was, the hero of the story, it was remade to be all the stuff writers love, and when it was your own story, you loved writing it more. It was awesome getting attention, and being the hero in the story. Writers are so often thought to

be just the recorders of history. To be a part of
history, sometimes that means everything to a writer.
It means everything to Holden. He was one of these
winy writers that wrote about relationships. That was
one of the problems with his books. Why did they love
him? What made him the hero? An objective instance
where he was the hero, was exactly what his books
needed.

But he needed to focus just on getting them out of
this. Right now he had to try to solve the situation
before it headed somewhere bad. But if he couldn't
stop the stalker, he had to make Fionae aware of the
situation, and her fear and emotion would be a factor
he would have to try to deal with so that they both
survive, and don't get hurt.

He heard a sound outside that sounded vaguely like something he had heard over the past few days. The stalker was out there again, masturbating. As he listened, the sound got a little more intense, and it didn't stop. It was there, and it was constant. You could even tell what it was.

He walked over to the window, the stalkers favorite one to peer through, and looked out, as if he was looking for nothing in particular. When he wasn't expecting Holden to be by the window, his eyes were often closed. And just as Holden expected, the man's eyes were closed as he was jerking off. It was disgusting. What was to be done about it.

Three

-

Suddenly a burst of emotion went through Holden,
and he all of the sudden felt courageous. He bounded
over to the door, and opened it and ran out onto the
balcony stairs, pouring down them to get to the
stalked as fast as possible.

When he got to the bottom, the stalker had pulled up
his pants, and was already running off into the
nighttime.

Hey, you fucking cunt! Get back here!' But the stalker kept running, until he was completely gone, and you couldn't see him anymore. He had vanished.

Four

-

Have you ever heard the worst killer in history outside

your apartment?

You had not. Because… If you had, you're dead.

You're dead now.

No one has ever caught the worst killer in history. No one ever will.

Now Holden. If only he was as dumb as his Goddamn girlfriend. But would they be together?

A dumb writer, hah!!!!!

Well, I'm going to make that you, Holden that's you.

I'm going to trick you out so bad.

And I'll fuck you too. And I'll kill you too.

That Holden. Holden. Damn himmmm!!!!!!!! How dare he fucking heard me. This. Is. The. End. Of. Him!!!!!!!

The End.

5

One

-

Salazar's office sat at the back of the law firm he had inherited from his father. The firm was quieter now, it was late at night. Past eleven. Salazar was still there, and Holden was visiting him now. The two of them sat at the desk, discussing in the most in-depth detail possible the sighting of the stalker and his flight, and every related element of the case. There was a definite chance they could identify the stalker now. They knew details about his behaviors throughout the entire day at this point, and they now had a description.

"He was tall?"

"He was 5' 10" or so, he looked fairly big."

"Was he not good looking?"

"I'm not sure. He was sort of far away. It was hard to tell. He looked good maybe, but it was too hard to tell."

"He looked good?"

"You know what I mean."

"I do. Well, alright." Salazar moved his hands over to a nearby document. He moved it to the center of the table, and motioned to it with his finger.

"These are all the locations we have seen him around the city. We had found he followed your girlfriend after the two of you were at a coffee shop, and from there we found that he is in fact stalking her as well. I am sorry."

"I understand," Holden said. "It is okay."

"Right now we have located him outside of her apartment, we have located him outside grocery stores she visits, salons she visits. Unfortunately, as of right now, we haven't been able to trace him after he has stopped following her. He disappears."

"You can't find his apartment, where he lives, is work."

"Unfortunately, we cannot. Though, based on just how much time he has spent stalking the two of you, I think it is safe to say he doesn't work."

"How much time?"

"Well, as you know, he has spent a significant amount of time stalking you. You have noticed him a lot of times, so you know about the exact amount already. I'm afraid he is stalking her the same exact amount of time."

"To be honest I had a feeling he was."

"He is indeed. Yes, in fact it has almost been the whole day he has watched the two of you. One or the other. As if he was part of your relationship. But as you know, he is not. Sometimes he has been outside your house in the night. While you were having sex, as if he knew about it ahead of time. Though, both day and night, he has slipped away without us being able to identify him."

"I am shocked. He's been watching all hours of the day, and he slips away without notice? What the?"

"Yes any time of day he could be there. Or outside Fionae's place. I have a question."

"Yes?"

"When you were at Roverio's Italian, you slipped out

the back I believe. You saw him following you?"

"Yes, Fionae and I had a quickie in the hallway, so we slipped out."

"I am afraid he was watching you. He was inside. He could see you."

"What? No!"

You will have to be more careful. He could be able to see you at any time. Especially in public."

"We were just trying to keep things exciting. And he'd been at her home, I didn't want him watching outside…"

"I know. It's alright. But just skip that in the future. Until this is over. But the question…"

"Yes?"

"When you saw him outside, which way did he turn?"

"I am not sure."

"Did he turn to the right?"

"I really couldn't say. He disappeared."

Salazar was ready to note down what Holden said, but when there was no definitive answer, he slammed his pen down.

"Did you see what side of the street he was on? Left or right?"

"Well, I'm pretty sure he was on the right. That's where I noticed him. I can't say which he went though."

"Okay, that's helpful anyways." He noted this down. Anything had mattered. Then he reached to the far-left side of his desk, and picked up another document.

"Now this one," he said. "It may frighten you. "Do you remember this?"

Two

-

He could recognize the audio. "What the? My wife was only blowing me in the bathroom. You said the cameras in the hallway had to be there… there's only some many times you can do it in the bedroom. But why?"

"I don't know. You see the mirror. He's slipped this device under the door. And he is jacking off uncontrollably, I have never seen someone beat off that hard ever. He is even bleeding. He has just a towel ready."

"I could not see the mirror at all. No… I completely missed it."

"It is okay. He knew you wouldn't look."

It was obvious he knew that Holden wouldn't look. "Unbelievable. He was in the apartment. I was just out of the shower… and he was watching like he was right there."

"I'm afraid that's right, Holden. So now that could be the case. Someone could be watching everything. You may feel very uncomfortable."

"Alright. I'll be ready."

Three

-

I know how you thought I would be going right now.

Like oh fuck yeah, oh fuck yeah? I am. Oh fucking

yeah. Oh mother fucking fuck yea. Wooo! Let get this

right in the ajar mouth. Oh fuck yeah. I grabbed this

bod a fucking month ago but because it's been in the

freezer its brand new. Yea all over teeth and the

gums and everything. Ahh ill still got a boner left got

get it right in the vag. Lady hold still hahahahahaha.

Ohh fuck yea.

Lady's not alive and she doesn't know it but her legs

are wrapped right around me, and I'm on a knee

pounded her with one else closed the other sneaking

at a peek at her half blue body. Those tits are perky

from the freezer, oh there are great things even in

death. I think I have some tremors. Right inside and

nothing is gonna happen. There. No little me running

around killing everyone around. I never killed the

people closes to me that's why I was never caught.

Then again by now. I fucking have!!! I lied!!! Jesus I need a fucking bat.

Beat that but. Agghhh. Beat it. Beat it. Is there any blood yet? Yea. Now fuck it. Oh that shits warm. Ahh I barely have a hard on. Ahh but I want it so bad. Keep going baby, keep going. Aggh. That's almost enough until later.

I can't wait until fucking later. You may not think this but I'll be back for you a fucking 30 minutes. I'll wait this time. And I'll be so fucking rock hard you're not

going to know what happened.

You never saw it fucking coming chilling at fucking

Disney Land, with your goddamn boyfriend. You find

the only god damn bar in the place. You trusted me

enough to go in that maze with me, see what

happens, then all of the sudden I am in your ass and

you're actually not that scared. Then I broke your

fucking neck, you don't feel anything. And I was

fucking you so hard I broke your fucking pelvis.

Probably half your vertebrae too and you don't make

a fucking noise. So one half hour, I'll just skip to

remembering that because I want such a big one. I

couldn't get that off the back of my mind, otherwise I'd

be beating right now and speed walking to your body.

You're fucking mine for an eternity.

Three

-

Holden is a little late coming over. But he had said he

was just finishing something up with his agent, so I

was totally not mad. He only occasionally makes me

wait. There was never anything to worry about. He is super loyal. And he always has a solution to everything. I think that is him now.

I did notice him knocking lightly as now he has text me that he is outside. Sometimes he does that, he only knocks lightly, so as not to draw attention to us before we fuck our brains out. We obviously are going to right now. I open the door to the hallway, and he is there. 'Hey, babe.' He comes inside and says, 'I am sorry I'm a little late.'

'I hardly noticed,' I said. And then I put my hands and his jaw and stuck my tongue down his fucking throat.

A couple licks of his esophageal sphincter and then I wrap both my legs around him. Next I undo his button, and his zipper, and his pants, and then I have his dick out and I'm jacking it off. He's getting hard for me and he is at six inches already. I want him inside already but I want the dick in my mouth first. I slide down him and I turn my head sideways, and I take the whole dick in my mouth at once. My hands never leave his waste. Now he's getting really hard and I can hear him deep in my throat in my ears, going back and forth. A couple minutes later and I'm so fucking hard myself I turn around, pull my panties down, and tell him, drill me in the ass, hun.

He's penetrating now and I like it so fucking much I'm feeling delirious. 'Fuck yea, baby,' I said. 'Fuck yea.'

It's been a while and I don't need to feel we're making love at all anymore. 'Harder,' I say. "Fuck me so fucking hard.'

He's fucking me hard now. I start twirling my clit, and I feel ready to come almost. I feel it all the way down my legs and I let him see me shutter. I moan like I'm in a fucking dream, and I'm getting fucked by God.

We need to take this to my bedroom, and I let him carry me with my eyes closed, my mouth on his nipple like he's the chick. I don't bite, but as soon as we land and bed I thrust his head down into my

pussy. I press him down little so he really eats it. And

I tell him to bite it a little, because it's that on my

mind.

Four

-

It's been five minutes, and that's enough I need his d

again. Groaning I go bring it up her. I just give it some

blow, fucking quick as I can, so he's ready to get in

my pussy and completely destroy it. At this point I

even thought to myself I don't need it my pussy. I feel

it stiff and I spit it out, and say to him, 'Destroy me.'

All of the sudden I am in the greatest place on Earth. I

just kept going fuck me harder, and I just said harder,

and harder. By the end I am in heaven, just me and

fucking him, and no one else made it. I am gonna

come now and the truth is I want to do it all on his

face.

I felt like I might become even like a slinky for a bit.

Then I went hunny, hunny, I'm going to come.

He's out of me a bit, I twirl the shit out of it, looking for

it fly sky high. It comes and a sec, and then I have

him licking it up. After a minute I have him all in my

mouth while I'm jacking him so hard I think he might

bleed. I can tell he's ready so I open my fucking lips,

and I just pull the thing as hard as I can, like it's all

stuck in there. Bam, it's all over my lips, and in my

mouth, and I actually love it. He fucking loves me,

and it was all worth it for that cum I had. I lick up

every bit and then I swallow it like it's part of a jelly

sandwich and then were all done and ready to get

back to whatever we were doing. Maybe we weren't

doing anything yet, but I have never felt so good and

whatever we do is gonna be so much better.

6

One

-

They don't fucking see me. They don't fucking see

me at all. I'm the ghost of the mother fucking century.

Earlier I took a shit and got all the shitty shit over my

hands. I put all in that dead bods pussy and fucked it

like she was coming dead while I thought of her as

alive. I talked to her and answered back for her. How

are you sweetie? I'm good. Are your ready to fucking

die? I that am, who is this. Then Bam! Even fucking

harder. She's coming back shit all over the place. Ah

I'm slamming it so hard. I think it's even in my eyes

now. Oh shit mother fucking yes. Oh holy fucking holy fucking holy fucking anal fucking holy anal fuckey fucking ho-ly. Oh my goddddd.

My favorite game is just to slap with my dick. I slapped her with is so many times I got to the point where it suddenly just burst open with blood flying everywhere, as if it was split in half of ever. But it wasn't and I stitched it up myself and just went over annihilating the dead bod over and fucking over.

Ahh they're getting to the bedroom I have to move a bit. She's gonna be getting some head I can feel it. In fact I'm gonna get up on the balcony for this one. Oh they're about to go for it. She's pushing his head down. He's moving with her. Now he's eating her pussy. Agh agh agh. I am tugging it right in front of the window. Agh, agh, agh. Yea you're not looking hahahahaha! Tug, tug, oh yes!!! We've got some blood. Now I'll tug even harder, harder. Oh fuck yes!

Now they're switching it up. She's putting his dick in her mouth. I know exactly what the shit it is. She want him hard as a rock so she can cum really fucking hard. Yea. Hmm this part isn't as interesting. Now his dick is in her mouth. Oooh I'd like that mouth dead. Damn. Uh agh aghaghaghaghagh. My eyes are rolling back in my head at this point. How fast is she going? I look and see she's going really fucking fast.

OH shit, the fucker see's me. The dude is looking

right at me, but he's looking away now. He's like

thinking about, he's gonna try and over it up to her

now. Hahahahahahaha. Oh fuck yeaaa. Tug tug tug

tug tug. Squeeze. Aghhhhhhh. Oh fuck yea!!!!!!!!

Now I am going to have to kill you Holden!!!! Of

course that was already the plan so no worries!!!!!!!

Two

-

They're finishing up. Cum shot!

Waaaaaaaaaaaaaaaow. Ahhhhhhh. Oh fuck yea. I'm

gonna ah ave one myself. Hahahahaha Holden

you're having sex with a guy. Oh fuck yeaaaa.

What's happening now, oh he's cumming. Oh her it

comes oh. Oh I fall to my knees hard. On the

concrete. Blood. Of fuckkk yessss. Aghggh. All of the

sudden I slap my dick on the concrete like I'm a

wrestinlign referee. Once more so God damnhard. I

don't even care if someone hears it. Yeaaaaaaaaa.

The stitched break and everything. Red waterfall. Yes

baby. The greatest thing on earth.

Uhaghaghaghaghaghaghagh.

Oh my god. Am I okay? I am hahahahahahah.

I can see they're done. I'd better run away. I think I'll

just jack the entire time I am running

hahahahahahahahahahahahahahahahahahaha.

Three

-

I miss when I was young, and my head was full of the
starry ideas of a life lived in quest mathematical
peace. The only pause to the silence was the
pleasing sound of love arising.

The only issues were the issues of politics, and the
only task I had was to make beautiful art, in words, for
all of the people of the society, to enjoy, and
appreciate.

As I had appreciated a good poem they could

appreciate… a thousand. A thousand original poems.

Right from the depths of my soul.

Right from the depths of Holden's, your present

poet's, soul.

Four

-

You'd never guess what I am up to now. But it's the most jack off-able stuff I have ever come up with it. See, I know it advance. But you're going to just have to see it come true. It is going to be fucking rad. Like my cum following from the sky all over your fuckers. Aghaghaghagahgahgah.

No one ever fucking know when you're stalking them. People are so fucking stupid you kill them on a sidewalk in Manhattan. Not you, readers. Not you. But my dick will be in all your orifices one day, at least in my opinion.

Is that not what you wanted to hear? I mean read on,

maybe this Asa will give you a nose job. I mean

dream on right. But you never know.

That guy's good.   A little too good. Oh yeah. Oh

yeah. Fuck yea. Aghhhhhhhhhhhhhhhh.

Five

-

Nah but in reality this was real life. So I was stalking

this three chicks as they're having their night out right.

And they think they're not going to get fucking

destroyed. It's your lucky night. Heheheh. That's right.

I got my eyes on you. I go up and I say I've got the

penthouse in front of Central Park and I own the

Lakers. In reality I killed the fucker that owns it but

they don't know that. They're roped right in.

Meanwhile no one know fucking anything basketball.

They just know the team in LA. So we get to talking

and I tell my favorite story. My groin hurts a little

because I got a bad strain trying not to get my dick hit

by a car. I was trying to avoid it, couldn't. But luckily I

thought to save my huge dick, it's huge right? You

can tell this is not true. I mean all of it. Anyways. I

serve and it just hits my groin, right? Misses my dick

by a hair. That's the story, you know? Anyways.

They're a bit drunk. Of course I have picked the right

time. All they really heard was big dick. Ladies' night

like that, they might have thought they'd drop ten g

just for a big dick. Anyways I getting to saying now, I

have a sixteen-inch penis, so that's why there was a

high chance of it getting whacked by the vehicle.

No one ever told a story more seriously either. I mean I'm all fucking in. In reality serial killers are the best actors there ever were. I have no emotions. No emotions whatsoever. Oh fuck yea. Oh fuck yeah. I'm jacking under the table but they have no fucking clue. No fucking clue at all!!!!!!!!!!! IN my head I'm just ah ah ah ah ah ah ah!!!!!!!!!

I have read all of the Mystery Method, obviously, so I know to get them to the next location right away. That's home. Not seriously. I killed the guy remember? But that's the private place where I'm gonna fuck the shit out of all three of em. Dead. See

how that guy sucked. You just had to fucking kill em'

to just slaughter every mother fucking hole in the

room.

Six

-

Are they ready to take the mother fuckin' plunge and

ditch this joint? With me. I gotta give em' something

good. Listen, I'm having a party up at my penthouse,

above Central Park. Just a few of the Knicks, a few

political types. Politicians, really. What do you say

you come up, have some champagne, spend some

time on the balcony. No strings attached.

Sure, they say. They thought about it a second or

something, but in the end I knew they couldn't wait to

get to the fucking party. They couldn't wait to be

above the park going ah ah ah rubbing their clits

while feeling better than everyone. That's a fact. So

here we go, I got em steppin' in a limo, tricked outta

their fucking minds. Little do they know as we're

driving off, the drinks I've gave them have a little bit of

ambient slipped in, so they'll be super docile and

compliant when we get to the apartment. We're

laughin' and laughin' I'm making shit up about The

Lakers, and Andrew Coumo and all this shit. I've even

made a few names up and they didn't fucking notice

in the least. This stuff is just a breeze. Nothing was

ever easier ever.

Here we are we're getting into the fucking apartment.

Going through the fucking lobby and shit. Damn right

I've got a fucking key. Damn right it works in the

fucking elevator. I killed the fucking elevator guy last

night, so I can just let myself up. Doesn't seem weird

at fucking all. You live on this floor, the top floor? Of

course I fucking do. I get off, the ladies are right

behind me. You can't hear anything inside, but that's normal. I stick the key in the door, unlock it, and step in. Come in, I say, as warmly as possible. They follow in, and I will never forget the slightly quizzical look on the ones face, the first one through the door. She never knew she'd die to a fucking dick.

And that's when I do it. I grab something I left on the table. A miniature sculpture of a dick. You know dick size. It's ceramic. And I shatter it on the first one's head. It shatters, but I still have along shard in my hand, which is filling with blood. And then I thrust the knife into the second one's neck, and slice it open wide. There's blood gushing out of her whole neck *like a geyser, as she falls to the floor screaming. The first one fell silently to the floor. Right after, I have my dick out. I pulled my pants down, grabbed it, jacked a little, and then I started killing them with it. Hitting them over and over with my dick. The thing is bleeding itself. It's getting purple. But I beat them, and beat them, until they mother fucking died. Then with is super swollen, twice as big as normal, I stuffed my dick in both their mouths, and fucked them until I had come six times in both their mouths, and I couldn't feel anything in my whole body I'd lost so much blood, except all the pain from the swelling, and high from the dead bod sex.*

After, you'd think I was done, you'd think that was it,

the grand finale. But it wasn't. I still wanted plenty

more from them. The whole night was ahead of us, if

you were the kind of person that doesn't sleep. Lately

I have been. It's been every night, I go hard as I can,

killing every mother fuckin' hot woman on the face of

the mother fucking earth. By the end it'll only be me

that had em' all. Once you've had, you might as well

not leave em' for someone else. After this, I tell you

I'm going to Paris and I'm going to sleep with every

super model and the planet and leave em' all dead.

Dead in the fucking ground. And full of my mother

fucking cum.

So I drag their bodies into the living room. I pop some fucking popcorn and poor a couple fucking champagnes. Its fucking New Year's baby, and I've get them both lying dead, on their bellies, heads tilted up a bit, their chins rested on their floor, watching the tv a bit. And it's the fucking best, every time there's a hot chick that comes up, I pop my dick in one of their eye sockets and fuck it stupid, while I try not to get any in my champee, and I take big swigs all the while get fucking wasted, before the ball drops, so I fuckin' celly so mother fuckin' hard, while I just fucking jump all over them. I'm not sure if im gonna spill any champ or not, meanwhile, I'm gonna started working' on their other socket, both of em' as soon as the scheduled

programming is over. Uh, oh, oh, oh fuck yeah. That's

what it's going to be like. I can't wait.

Seven

-

Sometimes things bother me too, not literally

everything is a party. I have my phone on the ground

in front of me and I pick it up and check on my

favorite friend Holden. He thinks I never leave his

side. Hahahaha. I almost never do. Though

sometimes there is someone else to stock!!! I

managed to leave a camera so we can try a bit of a

distance stalk-prey relationship, while I just take care

of a few things. I can see his pretty face in the

camera. Though not as pretty as his girlfriend, who is

going to be the first person brought back to life by a

dick to be killed again. I can't fucking wait.

Earlier his girlfriend took it in the mouth backwards

while hanging from his neck with her legs around his

shoulders. It was pretty sexy and I am definitely going

to kill him for that. Just kidding. I already knew that!!!

I'm going to kill extra gruesome for that, though. Then

it is just back to writing, or watching some tv.

Sometimes that guy has writer's block. I wanted to tell

him to jack, but then he would know I was watching.

Just gotta let it out. Every single last bit of stress.

Wooo. Then you'll feel better.

That's just my perspective. While it's the only one

that's worthwhile, he might tell you it didn't do much.

Did getting with your girlfriend get twice as much out?

It not fucking had! It not fucking had at all!

What a fucking prick. I was waiting while he's writing.

Did he have to rub not out? I had had to. Like thirty

times. But he doesn't know that. It's so easy when

you get your hands on his work. To fucking analyze it,

and read his fucking mind. It's because of that I can read his mind. He's so fucked because I just know what the fuck he's thinking 24 fucking 7. If he ever wanted to get away from me, he could buy a ticket to anywhere in the world, and I'd be there within fucking twenty minutes.

One time he went to the bathroom. I snuck in and came all over desk, while I was jacking on his chair. Oh my god some of this writing was so good. I got some on his chair, which is felt, but I wiped it up before it sunk it so he'll never know. Ah, oh oh oh, aghhhh. I imagined I was the writer there a bit, just writing a mile a minute, just fucking high on being so fucking good. Ah, oh oh oh, aghhhhhhhhhh. There

are something he'll never know. After that I slipped

out to the hallway of the apartment. In reality I

couldn't wipe literally everything up. I left little bulbs

on the edge of the carpet, up against the wall. If you

looked really closely, you could see them there. But

no one fucking ever will. Mother fucking agh. Aghh.

Agghhh.

Eight

-

On the way out I stopped at the vending machine. I don't usually bother with those. But sometimes I do for fucking fun. I place my magnet on top of the keyboard, and the things fucking malfunctions. I swipe the dummy card, three fucking things fall out. And I take em' as I head out, to loop around, climb up the parking garage, and then swing up the balconies to Holden's balcony. Sometimes I sit one up and just watch fucking everything from there. I put the shit in my backpack after I'm through the parking garage, and I'm at the top of it. And then I catapult up them to Holden's floor.

Pretty soon I'm sittin' up there, and I'm just jackin'

while I eat the chips and the two chocolate bars. Just

jackin' on and on, jackin' just on and on while I eat the

chips and shit.

7

One

-

Time to get the party started with these two. It's

fucking 11 50 and I'm horny and bothered for a fuck

as possible. Sometimes I am thinking if only I had two

dicks. I grab one and fucking pierce her cheek. A

whole swab of it, the size of a dick gone. Then I put

my dick in her mouth, hard as a fucking rock, and

then I put it through the new fuckin' hole. I can feel

her mouth damn good and it's rubbing' her tongue

and shit, and then I'm bringing the other one in. I stick

my dick in her mouth two. Fucking half it's in her

mouth, half's in the other chicks mouth. Then I'm pounded both of their mouths at once. The pleasure is fucking outrageous, and the power is fucking awesome. Literally two mouths at once, and two mouths fully at once. Oh fucking fuck yea.

I'm gay when I want to be. But this is maybe what I will do Holden and his twat girlfriend. Just fucking take em' both at the same time. Oh my god the pleasure from that is so fucking intense. And I am just going fucking cum. Ahh fuck it's right down the second one's throat. Everything left I shove in the first one's mouth. Fucking lettin' it fly right into her fucking throat. Oh my fucking god. It's the best shit ever.

I haven't had my fill so I do that fucking thirty times.

It's just the best fucking best thing ever. After that it is

nearly midnight and its time for the fucking finale.

I grab the fireworks I bought. They're powerful like

fucking black cats. Here we go. It's 11:57. I lite two of

em' and then shove one in both there arseholes. As

soon as they go off, and I'm fucking both their pussies

one after the other, as their fucking butts are

exploding, starting to flame and burn up. And I can

feel the fucking warmth as I fuck their pussies, it feels

so fucking good. And there's smoke coming out their

bums, they're shaking up and down and it adds to the

pleasure. Oh my fucking god. It's 11:59 and it's time

for round two lighting another two fireworks, and

shovel in their butts, and then bam, I am at it all over

again. And the clock is fucking ticking. Baaaaam!!! It's

fucking midnight, and I'm fucking the shit out of their

pussies. I fuck em' as quick as I can. Oh my god I am

so fucking hard. And now time for the grand fucking

finale. I walk out with one of them, onto the balcony.

And I stick her mouth on my dick. And the standup

right next to the railing. I lift her up, over the edge,

and then I just stop holding. She's just fucking

hanging off my dick, her feet flying in the fucking air,

nothing beneath her. I'm hard as fuck and I'm flexing

a little, and she's just right there in the air, hanging off my fucking dick with her fucking mouth.

Two

-

A little bit later on, I've fucked them both 300 times, and I need to get a move on after all the noise I've made. These dead bods are more than worth holding onto. Especially for the memory. This was one of the best dead bod nights ever. And there has been many dead bod nights.

It doesn't take long, and I've rinsed the apartment.

Like I even fuckin' care, I'm a ghost. And if you think I

got anywhere but inside them, yea fucking right! I

have years of practice with that. Then I've got them

both in suitcases, their legs folded up, their arms

crossed over them, and I'm headed to the car.

A half hour later, they're tucked away in the freezer,

and I am sitting down for a cup of tea and some

fuckin' toast.

8

One

-

Holden was not an investigator, though he was the one living the story. It was his life, when this serial killer came around and watched him. When the serial killer came into his home, and was in the same room. What were the chances the killer would attack? It actually seemed incredibly likely. Serial killers obviously stalk their prey, toy twitch them a while, and then make a move to kill them. It was many a night that Holden would awake, sweating, flustered, frightened, from a dream where he was right about to die at the hands of his serial killer stalker. In a handful of the dreams, Holden had died, and awoken after. Nothing had happened in these dreams, after he died. He had laid on the ground, where he had died, and gazed up at the killer, killing his wife, in every single dream except one. In the other dream sequence, he found himself already buried, his eyes open, looking up the coffin, unable to move, and not able to breath, before he awoke. And when he awoke he felt his breath move in and out, he felt his hands and legs moved when he moved them. And he marveled at the fact he was still alive, when it seemed, at least in his dream, the killer had already struck.

He was frightened every day of the serial killer who was watching him so closely. He often thought his life was hanging in the balance, it was only something he could barely choose to keep. The fear, the painful intensity of knowing someone was watching you, was almost too much to take.

But maybe, if he could find out the identity of the

serial killer, if he could predict his moves ahead, and get the police on him… maybe he could save his life. Maybe he could save the life of himself, and the life of his fiancé. That would mean everything to him, absolutely everything.

Right now there was no time to think about it anymore. Fionae was on her way over to fuck him. Was there anything she even knew. No, though she had wanted to spend every second together lately. What if this stalker was someone you knew? What if he served you coffee, or opened a door for you? What if he could get right into your life, and interact with you? …And you would not even know it? Fionae was just slightly more scared the last few times he saw her. As of yet she had nothing to say about it, anytime you asked how are you feeling, she said fine, or good. But she was scared. Holden knew the stalker was not just out there, but constantly up to something. He realized he was probably so good, you couldn't tell the way he was affecting you. It would almost seem there was nothing he had done.

Two

-

She opened the door. She had a key, though from time to she sang and waited for him to answer. And then she would grab his neck kiss him with all of her spit and tongue.

Sometimes after that they fucked right away. Today was like that, and she ran right in. She jumped into his arms, and he knew instinctively to catch her. Her mouth was buried in his mouth, while she unlaced her camisole. She pulled her bra off as quickly as possible, and got his head in between them quickly, and said mhmm. It was a prolonged moment, and then she was pulling her bell bottoms down hard, to get the dick in before she could think about anything but the heaving feeling inside her middle.

They were fucking after that, standing there, like they were warming up as lovers. Just another prolonged moment and then Holden was deep inside, and she was bouncing fast, up on down on his dick.

They almost wanted to get it off right there, and when they moved to the couch, it already been ten minutes since she walked in the door. But almost all of that had been after she let it penetrate her the first time.

She lightly guided him to lie down, and she sucked his dick, occasionally licking his balls, and taking one in her mouth, and flinging it around like a dog toy. She didn't bite, but you could see all her teeth half the time she blew him, and half the time his balls were in her mouth.

After that she rested her hands on the sofa arm rest, and held her but right up while he fucked her ass. They were deep in the throws, and she was saying fuck yes, and moaning, throughout the anal sex.

Then she took his dick again, and sucked as hard as she could, as if love could be expressed through intensity. The intensity of her passion couldn't be missed, and Holden felt deep in love with her. After he was going down on her, nudging it and licking it hard enough to make her come. And then she had her face down on the couch, while he held her, and took her from behind.

At the end, she grabbed his dick like it was her hubby, and used her hands to make him cum. At the moment it burst, he let the resistance in his body build, and then he came right her in mouth, and then got some on her lips, and she ate it all licking it up by moving her tongue around in a big circle, and then swallowing it all heartily. She smiled at him, and then he went down on her one more time, while she lay on the couch. She pushed his head lightly down to her pussy, and he ate her out. Until she came, and she was quenched as well.

Three

-

My love, my everything,

There isn't a moment I don't think about you. Was

that something to do with our bodies desire to have

sex?

I know that it wasn't. Never before has someone so

consumed my mind. And never has someone stolen

my soul. It is stolen because I gave it to you. And it never wants to come back to me.

And so I lend it to you Holden. For eternity. And if someone, there is even a second after eternity, then I lend it you then, and I lend it to you after then.

Four

-

A few minutes later they were laying on the couch,

with a duvet blanket from the bed draped over them. They had wiped themselves with Kleenex, I mean to say anything they hadn't eaten off each other. He lovingly caressed her hair, twirling it, and she dozed a few times, though woke up, having the thought in her dream, that she needed to kiss him, and she kissed him each time. After a while, Salazar need to go to the bathroom. Hahaha. I'm only joking. …Holden needed to go to the bathroom, and he moved her arm carefully from under his, and then set her body fully on the couch, and moved to the bathroom.

When he walked into the bathroom, it seemed it was occupied, because the stalker was in there. I mean, he must have been feeling a bit off, he was usually so smooth. But there he was on the toilet, masturbating harder than had ever seen any human masturbate, like online, or anything. He could only think, 'what the fuck…'. But quickly he realized he needed to do something. And he thought to be the first one to speak. "Hey," he said. "What the fuck are you doing?" By the time he said hey the once unstoppable stalker was already moving. He still had his hand on his penis, but had almost gotten around Holden. The stalker try to move past him and get through the door. There was some room, he had stepped into the bathroom a bit, if the guy could just get past his hip. And Holden was unsure if she made contact with the strange person, especially when he had his hand on his penis… But he thought about Fionae being out there, and he quickly moved to block the man from exiting. The stalker anticipated the move, and stepped around as far as he could. Holden almost had stopped him from stepping out, but the stalker removed one hand from his penis and punched

Holden away from him, as Holden was trying to body check the jacker into the bathroom wall. Well fuck, he thought, the stalker go through and was out the door.

The stalker ran to Fionae instead of running out the door, or one of the windows up the apartment. I mean it was long way down, but who knows with this guy. He grabbed her and pulled her to the balcony. But before he stepped up, and started jacking again. She was asleep, though it seemed she might wake up. He was jacking right over her head like he was going to come all over her face and hair, and Holden saw him. Suddenly he ran as fast as he could over to the stalker. One more body check, and the jacker crashed through the glass, and almost fell over the balcony. And he failed to ejaculate on Fionae's face.

She awoke startled. "Holden," She said, "Get him the fuck away from me!" Holden stepped outside, after the stalker to subdue him. But he still had much of the same slickness, and bounded down the balcony to the balcony below, and then he jumped down one more balcony, and then he broke through the glass door, and ran into the apartment, and likely ran off into the night, perhaps never to be seen again.

Five

-

Holden ran and took her into his arms. She was shaking badly, though she was alright. He had not hurt her, though the shock was very strong. "Hey", he said. "Are you okay?"

She looked right at him, she looked upset enough to cry for a second, though it passed. "I am," she said. "I'm really okay. You saved me. I can't believe that. But you really did."

"He not had hurt you. He had not done anything at all. But the shock of it? Is there anything you need?"

"You, I just need you. In fact, to the point of absurdity, that's all I need. Don't ever leave me. And don't ever not make love to me all day."

She got up from the ground, and kissed him very hard on the mouth, and then she held him in a hug for a bit. "Just want you to be right next to me with no gap ever."

He held tightly. That's all I want is for you to feel okay.

"Come lie down with me a bit," she said.

They went into the bedroom. They got comfy with the duvet from the couch, that Holden had brought back. She laid her cheek on his collarbone, and she closed her eyes. And she fell comfortably asleep, feeling very grateful to her lover.

Six

-

Holden stayed awake a little, and worried that the stalker could come back. He thought about how he had found the stalker just sitting there, and he wondered if he could have done anything differently.

There wasn't much of anything. And hindsight is 20/20.

There wasn't any reason to do nothing, so after a while, he went and locked the door. And then he went back to bed and slept as well.

It was almost four hours later that they woke up. It was Fionae that woke up first, and when she brushed Holden's face and woke him up, he opened his eyes, blinked, and saw her approximately a few inches from his face. "How are you feeling?"

"I'm feeling good. In fact, I'm feeling really good." "It looks it. You've never smiled so purely."

"That's now. And all I want is you."

He knew she was alright. And he trusted her deeply.

She leaned in to kiss him, and he grazed her neck lovingly. They were still naked and she climbed atop him, and massaged his penis to get it ready. And then she started having sex with him as lovingly as possible. She cherished every moment with him while they were in throes of passion. And each movement seemed to have the magnitude of all the love in the world to her.

Seven

-

They turned on their side, and she motioned for him to fuck her, and he also made love to her, going deep inside, and not going too quick. She moaned, and said yes, over and over. Soon she was saying harder, and harder. Then she went on top again, and started really fucking him. She made the decision to fuck harder than she had ever fucked. And she assumed Holden could handle it. With both her hands in the middle of his chests, she rode him like the wind. And with her hands between his chest muscles, it was like she was shocking him with panels back to life. By the end of it she was screaming at the top of her lungs.

She came and just kept going. Her orgasm got deeper. Until she came again. Then she needed Holden more. She went down on him and choked it all down and held it in her mouth for what felt like a minute. And then she bent over and told him to thrust as hard as he possibly could. "Fuck me, fuck me as hard as you possibly can." And he started going harder. "Even harder," she said. "Oh, Fuck YEAAAA!" she screamed. Soon she came, once more, as hard as possibly could. Over the bed while Holden was still inside her. She shivered and then stayed motionless with her eyes closed, panting. Then she turned around quickly, took Holdens dick, and beat it as hard as she could, almost like the stalked beat his, Holden thought. And she directed the cum all over her face. She loved the sex, and the pure passion with her partner, and there didn't seem to be anything else so important in the Universe.

9

One

-

Holden, my dear? Do your hear me?

I need for you to be able to hear me always.

And I need more than that. I need to have you here,

next to me, always.

I need you to hear every thought of mine. I need you

to hold me every time I cry.

I need you to be my husband. And I need to tell you something. I see him around the corner, though I can never see his face.

The stalker was there, moving in the same way. And sometimes, his hand is…

Right down his pants.

Help me, babe.

Two

-

They slept again after that, through the night, and until early in the morning. They awoke around 4 30 am, and found the apartment cold from having the window broken.

"I guess I should get that fixed right away," Holden said.

"Yes! Get it fixed right away!" And there was something else on her mind. "Holden who was that?"

"I don't know. It was nobody," he said. But there was more he needed to say. "It is possible we have a stalker. I don't know how to say this, but it is possible I have seen him before."

"Oh, no!" She said, as she grabbed him in her arms

and hugged him. He knew to hug her back. "I believe you, is it bad?"

He was not sure how much to say right at first. Though he obviously had to tell her everything. "You know, I think I have seen three, four times. It could be, and Salazar thinks it could be quite bad. They are sure he is stalking us, actually. They are sure it is often."

"Is it all the time? Oh my goodness?"

"I have to say Salazar says it is possible that he is. Though we don't know for sure. It is often."

"Nooo!" She believed him instantly. She knew someone was following her often. Whether it was all the time, she was too shocked to think about it right now. Presently, she just needed to try to process the truth that someone was watching her that she didn't know, and that he was trying to hurt her. All of the sudden, she could feel the effect she had had on him, how she shook a little before opening a door, how she felt her hair rising just a little time to time. That feeling of things not quite adding up. It was this person, this stalker, that would watch her... constantly, perhaps all of the time.

"It's Okay," he told her. "Everything is okay."

"What if he's around now? What if he's here tonight?"

 "I'm with you. He's not going to get to you ever."

"Holden, I am alone all the time. How am I going to live with this? How am I going to stay safe when there is a mad man doing all of that."

"Well, there is something I have to say. Maybe I should be with all of the time, from now on. I can protect you."

"Holden what if we got a security guard?"

"The thing is... I want to protect you. I want to be the one to do it. I will always be there for you."

"Well, okay. You are my love. I believe in you. You will keep me safe."

"Yes, absolutely, I will. I will until this is over."

"Then I am moving in."

"Really? I could always stay at your place."

"Nope, I am moving in. I just want to be right here. I want to make it as easy as possible for you, okay?"

"Well, okay. I am totally fine with that."

"And if we want to stay at my place for a change, one once in a while, I am not giving it up, so that's going to be alright."

"That's fine as well. And I'll keep you safe no matter where we are."

"Thanks, babe," she said. And she kissed him with grateful emotion.

Three

-

They got up, and showered together, and got in the car. They had bagels and coffee from a shop they parked at and went in for five minutes, eating them on the road. Holden dropped her off at work, and then drove to his writing office to try and really get some words written down, in spite of all of the torrid drama caused by this terrifying villain.

He watched her protectively, as she walked into her shoot, dressed in skintight jeans, and a leather jacket covering her shirt which exposed her large, and fake, boobs. It could make him feel like quite the writer, having her on his arm, or sitting beside him in every cafe, but right now, he just felt like the right man for the job, the protector of those in need the most. Right this second that was her without any argument that could deny it.

As he drove the streets, he looked around for their stalker, but he didn't see him. He felt certain this was only for a lack of intensity in his effort; the stalker was without doubt lurking just behind some corner. And he was lurking with the most passionate interest, and most evil intentions.

When he arrived at his writing office, he expected the most ordinary and routine experience, but he was going to have an exceptionally bizarre and unexpected one. There was no way of knowing; there was no way to prepare. But he would make it through… probably.

Four

-

He slipped through the door and everything seemed perfectly normal. But there was something he could not sense. Someone was not there. Someone was lurking behind every corner, as he drove through the busy roads to here, and he was already in the office.

Holden sat down at his desk, and opened his laptop and set to work. Certain element of the the past day animated his writing, and made it ready to flow from his fingers. In ten minutes he had the first page.

From there it is always tougher. Nonetheless, in

another ten minutes he was almost done another page. He was typing up the end of a great paragraph, when he felt the coldest finger he had ever felt touch his lips. Then he felt it forced into his mouth. The stalker would not let him push it out. So not knowing what to do, Holden bit down. The stalker's finger severed from his hand, the bond cracking loudly. But he not backed away. Instead he came inside Holden. He was jacking profusely with his other hand. Based on the grimace on his face, there wasn't much time left before the man came. And all of the sudden, he came all over Holden's laptop, and screamed, agghhh.

Something about it hurt so deeply, it was like someone had meant to grab his heart out of his chest, and rip it out. He could feel about the same amount of emotion watching the stalker's cum ooze down his laptop, as if he was watching his heart oozing blood, lying on the floor beside him.

The jacking attacker, suddenly brushed all the keys of Holden's laptop with his penis. But it was what happened next that was so terrible, and horrifying. In the blink of the eye, he grabbed the laptop, held it above head. And then suddenly turned, as if he had been studying where, and exactly how Holden had been sitting, the entire time he was writing, right over the head with laptop.

Five

-

When I was a child, I discovered masturbation.

I was four, and do not doubt me. I saw it on tv.

There was a porno as my Mom changed the

channels. And I felt it in my dick. I know I had.

Tell me, Mom, I said.

No, she said.

Come on, tell me.

It was a porno, it is not for you, she said.

So I looked it up. Then I watched porn every time my mom wasn't home, every time she was at the store.

And rubbed it. I rubbed my penis, and I rubbed it on and on.

Soon, it didn't whether she was there on not. I just rubbed it twenty-four seven.

She could hear me, and she would cry. After a while,

I didn't care at all, and I would beat as loud as I could,

and as hard as I could.

And she cried hard, I mean, she balled.

But when I hadn't quite had enough. I walked into my

Mom's bedroom and took my dick right in her mouth.

And I told her not to fucking move until I was finished.

Six

-

The jacking attacker had a nick name he liked to call himself. No one had ever jacked off on so many living bodies. No one had ever jacked off on so many dead bodies. And those were what he loved. Of all the jack offs, all the rapes, those were his favorite of all. The dead bod ones. So that's what he was. The "Dead Bod Man".   The best fucker of dead bods ever.

The "Dead Bod Man" had knocked Holden out cold. He had damn near killed him. In a heap, on the floor, he looked not like a champion writer, but a broken victim. There was no way that guy was moving for hours. The "Dead Bod Man" took down his pants, and started jacking very hard, just like he wanted to do if it was Fionae. He was squeezing his dick to the point where it bled, and jacking unbelievably hard. And then he came all over Holden's face, and hair. He shot some first over Holden's nose and eyes, and then over his hair, dangling above his forehead. The Great Writer, humbled, embarrassed, made nothing.

He wasn't done with Holden. He went to the kitchen area of the office, found the bottles of wine, and beer. And drank them. Two bottles of wine, three beers, done. Like that. Almost in a minute. Then he went back over to Holden. This time his pants came clean off. And then he kneeled down, spread Holden out, as

if he were lying on a very narrow bed, and then he
turned him on his back. He grabbed Holden pants
and ripped them down his legs. And the same with
his boxers. And then he stuck his dick in Holden's
butt. And then he fucked him as hard as he could,
while Holden was unconscious. The Dead Bod Man,
on top of Holden, raping him, while no one could do
anything about it.

This was one of his main two prey. He had followed
Holden and Fionae all day. And although he preferred
women to jack on and fuck, he was more than happy
with this one. As the boyfriend of Fionae, no one man
had ever obsessed him more. The Dead Bod Man
tried to ravage Holden's butt with all his might. Then
he stood up, and jacked as hard as he could. Then he

kicked Holden over onto his front, and jacked into his face one more time. "And I am fucking gay. At least a little!" He shouted as he ejaculated onto Holden.

Seven

-

If Holden were awake, this would be the most scarring experience possible. But he was not, and he would not remember. But the pain in his asshole, the feeling of semen on his face, would sting in his memory for ever. Those would be undeniable signs of the fact he had been raped. They were in the future.

The Dead Bod Man went out of the office and into the

hallway. He went in each and every office on the floor, and personally jacked off on every desk on the floor. It was a dirty mess, for a bunch of losers that cleaned this building to clean up. It was not his problem at all.

When he returned into the room, Holden was still lying on the floor, unconscious. The Dead Bod Man went to find some supplies to pack Holden up and bring him back to his hideout.

10

One

-

I never thought I would say, do you remember the

first time I was raped.

I suppose that is too my wife.

Dearest Fionae, in the future, perchance I say to you,
I am the victim of vicious rape. And. A vicious attack.
For a while there I was not myself.

Am I myself now? Do I look hollow? Is a part of me
still dead.

I know you cannot tell me the future, but do you think
you will see less of me?

Am I still who I was? And darling, I have to ask. Am I
still the man you love?

Two

-

Holden had been knocked out cold for an hour now. To the Dead Bod Man it seemed he would be out all night. But the reality was he was coming around. In just a few minutes Holden would be awake. Somehow the stalker killer had overestimated the strength of his blow, and Holden was recovering consciousness. Would the stalker return before Holden awoke?

Two minutes later, Holden awoke. His left eye opened slightly, and he saw he was on the floor.

Next, he opened both his eyes, just slightly, and he saw the dead bod man coming back. He closed them again. He noticed he was not tied up. He had a chance to get out of this. The Dead Bod Man had a large garbage bag to put him in, and he was coming his way. The Dead Bod man leaned over and started trying to scoop Holden into it. He was not armed. This was Holden's opportunity. He opened his eyes quickly, and struck the Dead Bod Man on the head. Although it was not with a laptop, it was payback. The Dead Bod Man staggered back, and Holden started to get to his feet. He battled against his feeling of wooziness, trying as hard as he could to not fall over. There was an unbearable pain in his ass. It felt damage, and he wondered if he would be able to poop. But there was no times to worry right now. He reached out and punched the Dead Bod Man right in the head. The blow was substantial, but the Dead Bod Man caught Holden's hand. He twisted Holden's arm, and then he took one hand away from his grip, reached for a lamp, and swung right at Holden's head. The impact this time could be catastrophic, and the Dead Bod Man's aim was dead on. Holden ducked, his butt hurting tremendously, and he swerved out as well. He moved to the left, and the Dead Bod Man's crushing blow missed. The laptop was there. Before the Dead Bod Man could guess it, he grabbed it, and slammed it down on his head.

The Dead Bod Man's eyes closed, and he collapsed onto the ground.

Three

-

Holden looked down at what he had done. But in a second he knew there had been no choice he had. It was okay. That was a serial killer. Right away he thought he needed to save himself. He needed to get the Dead Bod Man all tied up, fully under control, or he needed to get out of there. The killer was so uncontrollable, there was nothing you could do about it almost. He would obviously escape. So Holden decided he would just run. He left the office, running. He ran down the stairs, and out onto the street. He started walking. He walked a few blocks, found a cab, and started making his way home.

When Holden arrived home, he headed right to the shower. He began washing himself of everything the Dead Bod man had done to him. He had left his Semen, he had left blood, he left emotional scars that would last a lifetime. Standing in the beam of the shower, Holden began crying. And he cried, for ten minutes. Then he washed the tears away from his face, and stepped out of the shower with his eyes fairly red.

Four

-

Holden woke up the next day exhausted. He had

been able to sleep given the extreme stress of the situation, and the effect of deep tiredness that had on him.

There was something wrong this morning. He realized it was still only five o'clock. And he noticed a banging on the door suddenly. It was loud but intermittent. It was possible he hadn't missed any noises while he was waking up. But the person was aggressively, violently, trying to enter the building.

There was only one person who could be doing something so violent. Only one person who could want in right this second. There was no doubt... It was the Dead Bod Man.

Something occurred to him. He had fallen asleep almost accidentally. Where was his fiancé? She was not in trouble if the Dead Bod Man was here… but how had he been so self-involved as to not even check up on her? When he had promised to watch her all of the time? And there was something else. Something must have happened to her at the shoot. Because there had been no response from her. In the middle of mourning being raped, he hadn't noticed, that he had not heard from her. And he wouldn't, before he fell asleep, quickly and unexpectedly, from exhaustion.

Six

-

She was going to be alright. It must have been him the Dead Bod Man was truly after. And he was here right now. He had to think what to do. He had fallen asleep in his change of clothes after showering. A pair of sweatpants, and a tee shirt. He knew what to do next. He sat up in his bed, and all of the pain in his butt suddenly became too intense for him. His weight on his butt almost made him lay back down, but he had to get up given there was no time. Grimacing, he pulled himself off the bed, and steadied himself on his two feet, the pain just slightly better now. He staggered to his closet and found a jacket. He put on shoes next. He had been wearing socks.

He was just a little better on his feet now. He walked over to the balcony, and just as his front door burst open, he was opening the sliding door, and starting to descend the stairs into the city streets.

Though as he was reaching the first level of the apartment building, he heard the killer step out onto the balcony roughly, and then start to bound down the stairs. It wasn't going to be easy. He wasn't going to let Holden away except with his dead bare hands.

It was a fight to the death, and the Dead Bod Man would just have to die from jumping off a building, or getting hit by a car, while trying to catch up to him. That is what Holden figured, as he reached the ground, and started off running as best as he could, for a bus parked two blocks away.

Once he crossed the street, he looked behind him and saw the Dead Bod Man was just reaching the ground, and would soon be after him.

One more intersection, and then he was there. He

climbed the bus stairs, quickly raked four dollars out of his jacket pocket, and then walked to the back of the bus. He tried to cover up his limping as much as possible. As the bus door closed, the Dead Bod Man was just crossing the street, to where the bus was. As the bus began moving, the Dead Bod Man could be seen stopping on a pinpoint and running in the opposite direction. He was running as fast as he can, after the bus.

Holden turned around and watched horror as the Dead Bod Man chased and chased after him. This particular bus did not have so many stops. The next wasn't for ten blocks. So it seemed he'd get away. After three, four blocks, he could hardly see the Dead Bod Man anymore.

Seven

-

The bus stopped, at the next stop, and the Dead Bod Man could not be seen. While new passengers boarded, Holden felt so anxious he could about scratch a wound in his leg. But it wasn't too long before the bus doors closed, and the bus swiftly took motion again.

It was smooth another few blocks, but there was a particular jam at a stoplight. And the bus stalled.

Holden could feel it could even be a few minutes. He looked behind him. The Dead Bod Man could not be seen. The light turned green. But the bus didn't move. Traffic was stalled. Holden waited, and waited, wanting desperately for the bus to start moving again.

He looked behind him for the Dead Bod Man again. The bus inched forward. But it moved no more than that.

Holden kept his eyes peeled through the back window for the Dead Bod Man. So far there was still no sign of him. Surely he was running as fast as he could to catch up to it.

Then there he was, the Dead Bod Man. Conspicuously running after the bus as fast as he could. The Dead Bod Man was breathing hard.

Eight

-

As the bus stood still, Holden watched in agony as

the Dead Bod Man got closer, and closer. He turned around and saw that traffic was clearing. Car after car was getting through the intersection, while the light was green. As it turned red, the Dead Bod Man was still two blocks away. A quick light and they were through and on their way to the next stop still more than ten blocks away. Now he watched the light expectantly. Holden waited for it turn green. Second after second passed, and it wasn't turning read.

This couldn't be happening. Could it be real, that the Dead Bod man was this close to getting to him, in public, with nowhere obvious to hide? When the Dead Bod Man was so angry... It was the worst of circumstances.

A full minute and passed. And the light was still red. Holden looked behind him, and to his horror the Dad

Bod Man was on the block, and approaching the bus. He was running, running so fast, and in a moment, he was within ten feet of the bus.

Holden thought to himself, well what should he do? There were only two options, at least at first. Either remain where he was, and wait for the light to turn, or to run, and really try to get away. Which one was more of a gamble?

Nine

-

Holden looked behind him, but he didn't see the Dead Bod Man. He felt intense panic. Then he looked towards the door of the bus, the Dead Bod Man was right outside of it, almost close enough now to jump in. In a split-second Holden knew he had just to jump, and he went for it.

He sprinted for the back doors of the bus. He shook them back and forth, but they weren't budging. Finally he leaned all his wait on it. It busted just a little. He noticed he'd got the attention of the driver. 'Let me off,' he shouted. 'Please!!!'

In another moment, the bus driver released the door, and Holden jumped out and started running with all his heart. Away, away, from the Dead Bod Man that meant to do more horrible things to him, and finally take his life. As if he swallowed the key to the box with confession of all his darkest and most grotesque crimes.

It felt as if something ripped in his anus. And he knew
he was bleeding as he speeded along the sidewalk.
He just had to bite the pain. He kept running as fast
as he could. The Dead Bod Man had surely known he
had exited the bus, and was obviously in pursuit of
him. Was he close? Holden could not spare a
moment to turn round and check. Or maybe the Dead
Bod Man would catch up. To tell you the truth, he was
right behind him. He was three, four steps behind
him. If the Dead Bod Man jumped, he would miss
grasping Holden by an inch, and he knew that.

Holden kept pushing as hard as he could, through the
pain. He had lost a step, from the injury. But pride,
desire for survival, kept him running faster than he
could remember ever running.

Could someone chase him just as fast while only

desiring grotesque sexual conquest? Perhaps. And
while the chaser is not injured? It is possible. What
kind of shape was the Dead Bod Man? Not particular
good shape. He didn't exercise. At least not officially.
Though he spent hours, every single day, he spent
even half the day, just walking, stalking his prey. He
was oddly in shape. And was the Dad Bod Man
overweight? No, he hardly ate. But he had eaten with
a ferocious intensity, as you might expect. And if you
knew what he ate, then it would make even more
sense to you how the Dead Bod Man ate. He ate
dead bodies.

Ten

-

He was inching closer to Holden. And the latter sprinter could sense it. He tried to let go of all fear of pulling his limbs, all fears of collapsing, and just run like he had no ligaments.

Was it enough? Well, no. It was not enough, in the end, it was… not enough. But did Holden survive. Well, perhaps. But to tell you the truth, it is likely he might die.

A dead-end Holden swerved hard right, and crushed it around the corner. This was the advantage the Dead Bod Man needed. Suddenly Holden felt the coldest hand he had ever felt on his shoulder, and it ripped him backwards. He fell on his back. And suddenly he was at the mercy of the Dead Bod Man.

11

One

-

What is the difference between crunchy and soft?
Sweet and bitter?

Do you think I fucking care when all I tase is flesh?

It is like a seventh tase, the mother fucking taste of
tissue. Mhmmm. It was the best taste you could ever
imagine.

I was mother fucking addicted to it right from the start.
I would say if it tastes bad, I can't tell. If it tastes good,
I can't tell. But all of the sudden I feel so fucking good

inside when I am eating it.

It's a good year, by now, when I don't any eat fucking thing else.

They're all hung up in what I call the Hall Of Fame. So there's something to eat every fucking time I fucking sit down, and fucking eat something.

Two

-

What is the Dead Bod Man going to do to me? He is right above me. I don't think I can move in time. Will he use his feet? I think he might go for my privates.

But he is so angry, he may go for the face as well.
Either option might lead to me not getting away. I
don't want to lose my dick, but that way I will be able
to get up eventually, after the pain subsides. What is
he going to decide? Do I have any time to move?
I guess there's no time to wonder. I rolled onto my
right side and just kept rolling away from the Dead
Bod Man. He didn't kick me, but he bent down to try
to grab me.
The closest part of me to him was my feet. He tried to
grab them. After a few swats, he managed to get a
hold of my right foot. But something was happening.
We were in a public place. Onlookers, men, were
approaching to break up the fight. Although the Dead
Bod man was quite dangerous, they didn't know that.
It probably seemed to them it was almost a normal
encounter.

Three

-

Two men suddenly grabbed the Dead Bod man from behind, while he was unaware of them. He immediately swerved out of their grasp. The quickness of it, and violence of it, made three more men grab him. He fought back hard, trying to free his arms, kicking all around him. But the group of men got frustrated and threw him to the ground. When he kept trying to get up, they started to kicking him. But the Dead Bod man wouldn't be subdued. So one man kicked him right in the face to knock him out. He was dazed, but not quite knocked out. So the man hit him again, as hard as he could, and the Dead Bod man passed out.

Three of the men came over to me, and offered to

assist me. I worried that the Dead Bod man would

escape, but that was inevitable anyways. There was

no containing him. I feared he was probably already

waking up. Though the men were sure he was out

cold.

Four

-

"Are you okay?' One of them asked me.

I was gasping for air just a little bit. "Yes, I'm okay." I

needed to say something. "And thank you for saving

me. I need your help."

"Ha ha ha. It looked like you had it covered."

"No. The Dead Bod Man, you see. He's dangerous."

"The who?"

"The Dead Bod Man."

"I've not heard of him."

"He's the man I fought against."

"Ah okay I get what you are saying/ What does that name mean?"

"Well, the funny thing about it. He ahh… likes dead

bodies."

"How so? I have never heard of anyone liking dead bodies."

"He likes to hold on to them." I was going to say more, but an observer nearby said, "Hey, look, the guy's getting away!"

The Dead Bod man had gotten up. And now he was sprinting away. He had woken up a while ago, and he hardly seemed woozy by now. It was funny that he thought to run away, rather than come after me again. I suppose he just wanted to recuperate fully, before taken me on again. And maybe when these people *weren't around me.*

He was speeding away down a busy street now, and as he faded into the distance, he rounded a corner, and disappeared.

Five

-

I was sad to see him slip away, though there had been no way to contain him. The Dead Bod Man had not really lost so badly. He was always going to get up, and get away, before the police came to take him away.

Six

-

I told the onlookers, and helpers, that I was okay, and then I headed to Salazar's office. I called him and I told him about everything that had happened. It hadn't taken very long, and right after I told him that Fionae was missing.

"When was the last you heard from here?"

"When I dropped her off at a shoot, a few hours before the Dead Bod man attacked me."

"At your office, right."

"Yes, it was there."

"Well, if you're okay, I suggest we try to find her right away. I think I will give some information to the police. And by the time you get here, I will have had a chance to come up with a plan to find Fionae. How long do you think you'll be?"

"I'll be there in twenty minutes."

"Alright, I'll be ready by then. Byc."

"Bye."

Seven

-

Holden arrived at Salazar's office a little more than twenty minutes later. They met together in the back office, at a table with bundles of documents on it.

Salazar said he had given the police any information they needed to make the public aware of the Dead Bod man, and he also informed them as to the disappearance of Fionae. He had questions for Holden. They went over just like last time, every place he had seen the Dead Bod man.

"Since the last time I asked you, where have you

seen the Dead Bod man?"

"Everywhere. He's been stalking me the whole day."

"In your home?"

"Yes."

"In your office?"

"Yes."

"At Fionae's home?"

"Yes."

"Okay. So pretty much everywhere. I know you've seen him at restaurants, when you are out around town. Okay."

"So what are we going to do."

"I think we are going to wait for him. He will come eventually. He may sense us around, but he's too eager right now to wait. I would say within a few days, you will hear from him for sure."

Eight

-

"Okay, so you'll wait with me?"

"No, we will all wait outside. I'll be right in front of your building. But what he won't know, is that there will be another car around the corner. And when he goes after you, we will outnumber him. Right away we'll have a ton of guys right inside. And we should be able to take him."

"Well alright then, that makes sense. I think we can beat him."

"Well that's not precisely it. See it all sounds too predictable right. What if we have extra guys, you know? So we'll follow him back to where he goes. He'll obviously get away. And there, will find Fionae."

"Okay, this will work. I'm sure we'll find here, if we can just track him."

"And from what I have studied of the previous disappearances, when we find her, she'll be… alive."

"That's exactly what I wanted to hear."

"I know, and she will be alright, completely."

"Let's get to it."

"Aright, I'll set the plan in motion."

Nine

-

When will come for you?

The Dead Bod Man comes when he wants to come.

Whenever the Fuck he wants to come.

And don't worry. I know you are. He'll come for you.

You aren't going to be left out. If you thought that.

Lots of people had.

But I won't forget you. And I won't forget, to fuck every one of your holes.

And I won't forget to kill you and leave you fucking dead.

The Dead Bod Man is going to get everyone.

12

One

-

And the Dead Bod Man was no longer just a veiled myth or a whisper on wild winds, but a living, breathing, phenomenon. It was on your tv, it was on your phone, in your car. Someone had to speak to you about it at work... So if you see the Dead Bod Man... (RUN!), So no woman can be left to walk alone at night, okay? All over the United States, people went about their business cautiously, protecting women around every corner, and locking every door and window all day and night. Who knows where he could be... and that was part of the mystery.

693 murders were recorded all across the United

States, over the past eight years. Suddenly deaths in on state were connected to ones three states away on the next day. One of the most brutal deaths of all time, a man hung from a pole by his penis stapled to it, until he fell on his head and snapped his neck, was found to be the Dead Bod Man. He was not the indisputably the most infamous serial killer of all time.

Some serial killers were suspected of dozens they were never proven to have committed, but the Dead Bod Man was found to be the murderer of all of his suspected cases right away. DNA sample after DNA sample taken from the crime scene, in Holden's office, from the Dead Bod Man matched up to a hundred cold cases. For everyone time the Dead Bod Man jacked off, that was one more time he was close to getting caught. Who knew? No one, and his hubris would ultimately ruin all of his fun. One day. Today.

Holden was sitting around in his living room, with the bodyguards Salazar set up for him, watching the news, seeing for the first time, the Dead Bod Man identified and analyzed. Stories ran about what he had been like in childhood, what had made him want to murder people, what his first murders were like, it was shocking. The most gruesome and twisted serial killer of all time was now on television. Some people assumed he'd be brought in soon. Others assumed he might get away, and murder just as many people, all over, but somewhere else in the world.

One thing was constantly on Holden's mind, and that was finding Fionae. She was the most important person to him, and he would give anything to have here sitting next to him right now. But she wasn't. And she could be dead. Salazar thought she was alive, and a lot of analysts on tv thought she was alive. And

Holden secretly thought she was alive, as well.

Passing the hours was difficult. When he wasn't watching the news about the Dead Bod Man, he just surfed through the channels. He felt too bothered to watch the ball game, and he watched a bit of a few programs, before he began to feel everything was so boring, he was soon going to see a commercial for "The Dead Bod Man," the movie. He turned the tv off, and sighed deeply. It was disappointing to not have any way to comfortably pass the time, but it was late now. He could just go to bed. Of course, he went straight to bed. For a while, he laid awake and thought over the situation some more. But it seemed to him, after not very long, he was thinking over the same things, and he went to sleep.

Two

-

The next morning, he found himself well rested, he'd had a good sleep. There wasn't really any sign at all of The Dead Bod Man. It seemed things would be normal for a little while. He hadn't really much of an appetite the night before. He thought'd he set to it. Cooking up a few eggs.

He opened them up and spread them on the pan over some oil. While they cooked he took some bread, and toasted it to go with the eggs. While he waited for the eggs to cook, and the toast to toast, he noticed how quiet and tranquil the area was, just like no one expected the Dead Bod Man to come around. No one except him.

They did not need to be informed. It was just something for him and the security to know about. The amount of panic it would cause, would be astronomical. The eggs and the toast finished cooking, and he put them on a plate, and sat down at the kitchen table.

He began eating the toast first. He took a few bites of it, and then began on his egg. On the first bite of it, he felt a cold hand on his neck. Before he could even move, the Dead Bod Man threw his neck sideways. Holden passed out instantly.

Three

-

The securities sat outside the apartment, on the surrounding blocks waiting for something to happen. One was stationed on a hill a black and a half away to view the action in the apartment. He focused his binoculars. Holden was eating something.

Something was happening finally, as he suddenly disappeared from sight. He peered deeply, knowing that the next few moments of action were important. Behind Holden, or where he had been, he could see the Dead Bod Man standing, possibly with his hands on Holden. "Let's Go, full motion," he said quickly. "Holden is down possibly. And Dead Bod Man inside."

"Dead Bod Man inside?"

"Affirmative."

"Okay, let's go." He made a call on the radio to have all units head inside. They made their way inside as well. They were the closes group, and they made it inside first. They bounded up the stairs, and made their way to the door of the apartment. It was open, as Holden had left it. There was no saying if the Dead Bod Man went through it, although with him, I t was usually the window, or a ceiling panel. They rushed in.

They found the Dead Bod Man masturbating again. He was violently jacking off his penis right above Holden's face. Holden was across the breakfast table, his head laying on its side.

The first one in the door made their way to the Dead

Bod Man, and tackled him. They fought hard. He was unable to subdue the Dead Bod Man, and as other guards stepped into the kitchen, they blocked the Dead Bod Man as he tried to run away. One particular guard had gotten into such an intense fight with him, that he himself was clawing at the chest and arms of the Dead Bod Man.

They turned upon their sides and wrestled with each other. One guard had found himself atop the kitchen table. Full of desperation, he leapt from the table, and with all his weight, landed on top of the Dead Bod Man. He put his elbow to the Dead Bod Man's head as he fell. The Dead Bod Man passed out cold.

Immediately they turned their attention to Holden. With the Dead Bod Man, if he hadn't killed you, he generally knocked you out. So they had smelling salts ready when they arrived. A guard knelt down and waved a smelling salt beneath Holden's nose, and after a minute, he woke up.

When he seemed to be aware of his surroundings, they told him he was safe. He had survived, and the Dead Bod Man had not raped him.

They had not forgotten about the killer, and they all turned their attention to him now. The Dead Bod Man often escaped in a second, and this instance was going to be no different, except with careful measures. The guards had prepared a sedative so the Dead Bod Man could not run away, and they readied the injection now. It would work instantly, and it would be most potent right at first. All in all the sedative should keep the Dead Bod Man not moving for two hours. They administered the shot.

The Dead Bod Man was already not moving, though it seemed he might have gone a little limper. The guards, given their scientific knowledge, thought now would be the optimum time to confer and discuss what to do next. They gathered in a circle while the killer lay there unconscious.

They discussed how to get him to the police station, and ultimately into jail. They discussed whether to call for any help from anyone. They discussed eta to the police station, and to their home base, to prepare for whatever came next.

When they broke from the meeting, they noticed that the Dead Bod Man was already gone.

Four

-

The security guards did not know what to do. How on earth could someone make off while fully sedated? It made no sense whatsoever. For a while they panicked. Eventually though, they realized this was to be expected. They were prepared beforehand to know that the Dead Bod Man may slip off at any time, and in some way that was almost explicable.

Holden was shaken up by the event. This was the second time the Dead Bod Man had slipped away, when he was virtually right beside Holden. Both times were immediately following him attacking Holden as well.

The securities didn't know what to say to Holden, but

they had to say something obviously. Well, look Holden, he got away, as per usual. We had him for a minute.

It is okay, Holden said. It was to be expected, for sure. Well, look, The plan was to follow him, right.

Well, yes these were the units outside. They are. We have the information they are still behind him, they have his position.

Well we should get going.

I think wherever he is going, he is going to be there a while. It is his base, based on where he is driving. Way out of town. This was always sort of the plan.

Well, alright.

Five

-

Did you ever think you caught the devil?

Did you ever think you caught the Dead Bod Man?

The answer to first might be, no.

The answer to the second had better be, hell fucking no!!!

How the FUCK do I do it, I always mother fucking get away, OH YEAHHHHHH!

Crowd over here, cheer for the mother fuckin' DEAD BOD… MANNN….

Yea, Oh Yea… Fuck Yeaaaaaaaaa!

Now crowd over there, you cheer for the mother fuckin' DEAD BOD… MANNN….

Yea, Oh Yea… Fuck Yeaaaaaaaaa! Fuck Yeaaaaaaaaa!

It's been a million times I got away and it has been a

million time I got right back to it?

How did I do this time?

Ain't nothin' the Dead Bod Man won't shove in his

vains!!!

I am immune to everything, to every poision there

ever was, every one ever invented!!!

Come and catch me now!!!!!!! Rarrr!!!!!!!!!!!!!!!!!!!!!!!!

Six

-

Holden and the securities got into the vehicles and began pursuit of the Dead Bod Man and the other units. They should arrive to the hiding place in time to assist them in apprehending the Dead Bod Man. They may or may not be successful in that, but the main goal was to find Fionae anyways. Capturing the Dead Bod Man, in his own element, seemed impossible. Especially considering he would likely get away afterwards anyways.

Nevertheless, the made their way to the Dead Bod Man's hiding spot, while getting occasional updates about where exactly his hiding spot was located. It was the difference in driving North or North-West, or trying to direct themselves a little more between those two.

After forty minutes of driving, they were out of New York, driving North, and apparently approaching the hide-out. The location they tracked him to was another fifteen minutes drive from where they were. It was not what you would expect. It was not a house, or some sort of cabin. Rather it was recessed into the ground, with no entry but a few wood latches.

The other guard owned vehicles were there. They had hidden their vehicles, but were parked in front of the manholes. They were just waiting for the other guards and Holden, before they would burst in for an attack.

The others arrived, they were ready to jump into

action. One guard signaled to everyone it was time to go, and then they got a move on. Mines were set on both doors. A break into some sort of bunker or vault was expected. Five, four, three, two, one. The mines exploded and both latches were blown open.

They jumped in. Holden filled in behind them, keeping safe. His secret purpose, if he had known it, was to see Fionae down there, and alert them to it, and remind them to save her, in the midst of them fighting the Dead Bod Man. They thought about telling him this, but they figured it was better he just realized it on his own. He was for sure going to be just searching for her, and of course he would point her out to them in a second.

On the bottom, there was dirt floor, and a maze of doors and rooms. They began throwing each door open, searching in every room for the Dead Bod Man. Eventually they pushed further through the tunnels, before they came to something of a compound.

There was a wall built from cut down trees from the forest surrounding the bunker. A large door, like something taken off the hinges of a stately home, stood in the middle. It was probably a cherished relic of the Dead Bod Man, but all the same the crew of guards got to work placing explosives all over it. They instructed Holden back, and they all moved several meters back, as they got ready for the thing to blow up.

One, and two, and three. The door was obliterated, and all but gone. And all the guards rushed in, with the alacrity to catch the greatest criminal in American history, and save the princess of his sickest obsessions.

They entered a dark room, wide in size, with more doors all around. On the wall at the back of the room, was a large screen tv. It replayed the Dead Bod Man's greatest hits – his most gruesome murders, and his more grotesque sex crimes.

The guards began frantically searching every room, from near the entrance, to the back regions of the lobby. They came up empty through the first half of the rooms. In the latter half of the rooms, it seemed they would find something. There didn't seem to be anything else down here, in this god forsaken place.

There were two rooms right in the back, aside the tv, that anyone would inevitably come to last. It happened quickly, and rumor has it all of the guards

were in therapy for weeks afterwards, and the future
could see them in therapy for years, and years. In
one room, there she was, the blood leaking from her
like her life dripping away second by second. She
was barely hanging on, and her head was meekly
hung upon her breasts, like she was already dead.

And in the next room, the Dead Bod Man was hiding.
When they entered, he shot two guards, before a
third guard shot him. It hit his shoulder, and they fell
to the dirt floor after.

The guards were hit in the chest, and luckily, in both
instances, there body armor was not pierced.

This time they coiled up the Dead Bod Man, so that
he would not run away, at least not so easily. They
administered another sedative, even though it hadn't

worked last time. And for added measure, two guards pulled up chairs next to him, to watch him.

Seven

-

Holden ran to Fionae. His love seemed in great distress. To his dismay, she smelled, though mostly of blood, and he held her in his arms, as her eyes were barely awake. She shook a little, as if she was. She tried to speak, but she was too weak to say anything. You could swear she was whispering, but whatever she said was not understandable.

He held her close instead, despite her stench. He noted several wounds, and pointed them out to the guards to be healed up.

He noticed disturbingly that there was cum at the top of her shirt, and along the top of her breasts. He also noticed there was cum around her eyebrows, and some along her forehead. The poor thing had been having The Dead Bod Man jack of on her face. That was something they figured, though it was shocking to see he had really gone that far. He had even ejaculated on her face. He'd mention to the guards to give her face a wash as well, and hopefully that will help her feel a little better. Though it was tough to tell if she would notice.

Some guards came over to offer some care to her, and Holden let them take her, and he watched them take her away, feeling solemn and upset over what the Dead Bod Man had done. He wondered what she would remember. What would be the total amount of devastation, of things remembered, and things unremembered?

A guard wiped her face with a wet cloth, and then went over it with a paper towel, cleansing the ejaculate over her face. Another guard began cleaning her wounds with disinfectant. After that, he began sewing several wounds, so that she would not begin to bleed again.

The last thing they did was start an IV drip, with just a bag, and they pumped fluids, and vitamins into her. Once a minute or two had passed, she began to show the first signs of strength.

Holden was not sure what to do while she recovered, and the Dead Bod Man was being watched. He really had nothing to do. Instead of standing around, he walked back through the bunker, looking in some of the rooms they had searched. He found torture devices. Clamps that held your mouth open, bats with metal spikes on them, corrosive sprays that would melt half your foot in a minute. The Dead Bod Man was an expert on torture.

He didn't really have any real hobbies, but in some of the rooms were scrapbooks. They contained images of women, at least a few of each one alive and dead. They had large items stuffed up their anuses, they had boobs removed and sewed onto picture frames. They were tortured in a myriad of ways, and it was disturbing to look at, but it allowed Holden to estimate what the Dead Bod Man was like with his victims, especially over a longer time.

On some of the chairs was a single spike, and if a
victim sat on it, it would go right up their anus,
perhaps to their rectum, and rip everything up. He
could imagine the Dead Bod Man putting victims
down on the chair, and then fucking them violently
while their butt was mashed into pieces of tissue.
Along the walls, higher up, hung gallows like items, to
hold victims up by the necks, and most of them off the
ground, while he raped them from behind.

For a minute Holden couldn't catch his breath, he
stumbled, almost passed out. But he told himself it
was okay, and the Dead Bod Man hadn't done these
things to Fionae, and he tried just to forget all of it,
and try to focus on something positive. He thought
he'd go check on Fionae again. She would likely be
more conscious now.

But somewhat to his surprise, she was passed out, on a blanket, with her propped up on a pillow. He sat down beside her and held her dirt-filled hand in his hand. To have her next to him, filled him with comfort. He could see she was physically okay. He dreaded the stories of the Dead Bod Man's torture. He hoped she would be okay psychologically, but there were obviously things that happened, that she would need a long time to recover from.

He closed his eyes, and tried to really relax. What would happen next? Life was full of surprises when it involved the Dead Bod Man.

Eight

-

Right then, he heard commotion. There were shots fired, there was a tussle. Bodies being tossed back and forth, pushed and shoves. And then someone was running through the door adjacent to the room he was sitting in. He was pounding off on his feet. Of course, it was the Dead Bod Man.

Holden got up quickly, and looked around just outside the door. Guards were chasing after the runner, and then Holden looked towards the runner. It was definitely the Dead Bod Man, and he had almost gotten away now.

Another time, the villain of the century was slipping away, disappearing only cause horror and trauma in another place, in a time not far away.

Although all the guards chased after the Dead Bod

Man, there was no chance of catching him. He escaped through the hatch, and took off on a motorbike. Two cars of Guards quickly followed after him, though he had approximately escaped.

The remaining guards ran their hands through their hair, or grasped their neck muscles, expressing deep exasperation. The fucker was gone, they said. Again. They told themselves it wasn't on them, that he just always got away. But it was on them. No, I'm just kidding.

Holden didn't really want to complain. It was perfectly normal for a criminal like him to slip away. Maybe even from top police forces.

What had happened? Turned out they hadn't been watching a chair with a spike on it. The Dead Bod

Man was able to kick two guards in the head, one after the other, in quick succession, and then he crawled over to the chair, and freed himself.

After that, he was out of the building and on his way. There was no catching him now. What would the world hear next from the Dead Bod Man? You could only fear the worst. He could be pillaging a whole town, raping hundreds of women, all in the space of an hour, in one place along the highway, or another place, or perhaps in all of them throughout the night.

He decided he might as well get the hell out of this hovel. He navigated the dirt paths, and rose up the ladder to the ground, and emerged looking around, unable to see the Dead Bod Man at all. He couldn't see a vehicle chasing him, and he couldn't hear one. He most certainly could not hear the Dead Bod Man's motorcycle.

Nine

-

In the aftermath, there were many things going on. For Holden, he just wanted to know Fionae was going to be okay. The only thing he hoped for other than that, was for her to be herself again. He wanted to spend time with her and help her feel better. He wanted to help her feel loved.

But there were so many people swarming around, there were so many experts, so many counselors, that demanded every second of hers… when they weren't demanding that she sleep, and rest, and let the medications work. Too many people need to expertly help her, for love to have a chance to heal her. But it was no matter, he could wait, and when all this was finished, his time together with her would be so much more worth it.

For Fionae, she had experienced a numbness. Every second, someone was asking her for the full story, or they were asking her to prepare to give the full story. But she was not ready, and she often wondered just who to tell.

Meanwhile, she did sort of remember. She had been raped. She had been sexually tortured. He had singed her private parts, tore them open, twisted and pulled them in very painful ways. It was tough to think about getting into that, never mind trying to remember everything she had forgotten, all of the things that were likely even more painful.

Maybe after a number of years, when all of the things she did remember no longer bothered her so deeply, she could consider trying to recall some of the things she thought maybe had happened. But that was long in the future. It didn't seem to her anyone could her right now. It wasn't news reporters that wanted to know about it right now, but surely everything would come out with a trial. But Fionae would not be able to remember most of the things until after it ended. So, people would have to wait for the story of the Dead Bod Man.

As a therapist looked at her in anticipation of what she would say, Fionae felt hopeless, there was nothing she could say. She moved her mouth a few times, looking for words just a bit, and the therapist

had pen to paper, looking for anything to write down.
She wanted to find something in the mouth
movements, but she could not think of any word that
could have come out of the mouth.

Later a doctor checked up on her wounds. There
were lacerations on her legs, and he found the last
stitches were ready to come out now. The other bad
injuries were on her private parts, and he would not
be checking those today. Physically she was in a lot
of pain, she had told the doctors about it, but there
was nothing they said, except to get bed rest. They
seemed to feel the pain just amounted to whiplash.
She would have a lot of bed rest, until they feel the
psychological issues were something they
understood more.

13

One

-

I fucked her and I mother fucking fucked her,

Until nothing, until I wanted to fuck her some more,

Then on to her butt, then in her butt again, and on her butt while my cum

Is drizzled over it, then in her butt while he blood is fucking everywhere,

Maybe this time I'll save it for later, leave the butt intact,

But another time, maybe next time even, that will be

gone,

And in that way, it will mother fucking always be mine.

And you'll remember who the fuck raped that butt,

and who the fuck

Took that women in a fucking million ways, and

eventually took her fucking life.

Every victim's life ends like a fucking victims. It ends

with them fucking dead.

Two

-

For the first few weeks, Holden was there is the hospital for her every second. But after a while, he found it wearing on him. He was sleeping on waiting room chairs. Someone would bunch three together, and then give him a pillow. Though of course, sometimes he slept sitting up. And it began to wear on him that there wasn't a shower there, and he could not change clothes. That he had a smell was a truly unfortunate side effect. He knew it could not go on. He had to start spending time at home, and as much as he was reluctant to do so, he needed to start sleeping at home again.

Today Fionae wasn't feeling extremely well, so he saw her later in the day. He explained carefully, that he would have to spend some more time at home now. But he would still be her virtually all the time. All she said, was, "Okay."

And after that, he headed home for the first time. At least, to spend time there. Previously, he had only dropped in to grab some clothes, or maybe to take a quick shower. Other than that, he had been just at the hospital. He used his laptop there, he ate at the cafeteria, he used the bathroom there. He read the newspaper there. He was only there.

Well, the first thing was he took a bit of a longer shower. It actually felt very relieving. He could feel himself getting cleaner. There was a caking of sweat, and dirt, that he regretted. But it was being washed off. Afterwards, he changed into some clean clothes, ones he hadn't worn in a while.

And he sat down, and ordered something on Doordash to have for dinner. He turned on the tv, and watched the news. There hadn't been much on about the Dead Bod Man lately, so he figured it would be okay.

Three

-

He thought a lot of whether Fionae would get better, and a lot about what it would have been like for the past few weeks if he was here. It was well worth the trouble, he thought every time he considered which was better. You might say it was just interesting to think about the other side of things.

After he had watched two, three hours, it was late. It was almost eleven, and he could feel that he was really tired. So he went to bed, undressing, and getting in the sheets, all without setting an alarm. And he slept at home for the first time in three weeks.

Four

-

He woke in his bed, for the first time in a while, though it is many times in life we rise from our own beds. Everything felt the same, but he felt this was a different segmentation of his life now. He thought maybe chapter was a word with a more positive connotation. Well no, that was how you'd put it, he thought. It was a new chapter.

He got up to go about getting ready, and get to the hospital. It'd been a long while he had been separated from Fionae, in comparison to the infinitesimal amounts of time they spent apart while he was there in the hospital. He looked forward to being right there with her again. He hoped she hadn't felt alone for a minute. And he hoped she would see, he would always be there for her right when she needed it.

After he had some cereal and juice, he took off, stopping at CoffeeAmorous, getting a latte, and he arrived at the hospital twenty minutes later.

He greeted the receptionist, and walked up to the area Fionae was resting. It was just an area for long-term patients. She wasn't in need of acute care, though her needs did meet the demands of the kind of constant care a hospital could provide.

He found her not being attended by any doctors, or nurses, and in fact one out front told him it would be okay to go ahead and go inside. She was actually awake, this morning, and the tv was on. She was only watching morning show type programing.

"Hi." He said.

"Hey," she said.

"I promised I'd be right back. I hope you weren't alone too long."

"No. I've been asleep. It made no difference."

"I got you a cappuccino if you'd like."

Sometimes she took a beverage, or a sweet, and just

left it there, not having an appetite. Lately she grabbed it though, and had as much as half.

"Hmm. Sure hun." She took the coffee beverage, took a small sip, and set it on the table."

"How are you feeling today?"

"Well, about the same, you know. To tell you the truth, I hadn't mentioned it, but I feel a little less pain in my legs. Maybe in a couple weeks, we could go on a walk. I might be ready. And I would like that."

"A walk. Yea? Well, alright. I'd love that."

"Thanks, babe. That means a lot to me. Is it okay, if I have to sit down for a moment, too?"

"Of course, all I want to do is spend time with you. That Is all."

"Thanks. Then I think I'll be able to go for the walk. It will be the sweetest walk ever. You will be with me. The sun will be shining, except for a few clouds. And I will hear birds chirping, and water running through the stream, and nothing else, except the rustling of your shirt against mine as we hold hand, walking.

"I would love that. Then we will go for the walk. Well you seem a little better today. Though love can overpower us all."

"I do feel a little better. Just a little. And the first thing that came to my mind, and the only, was spending time with my love, you, and not anything else.

Then we will spend lots of time together.

Five

-

Can I feel my legs. Well, I can.

Can I feel my arms? Well, I can feel them. I can feel them.

Can I feel my heart. Truly, I cannot.

If I could take it out and look at it, my heart, could I inspect what's wrong with it?

Perhaps?

Would that confirm it's there?

I am not sure I know that – that my heart is there, that I am fully alive.

Do you know a part of me feels dead? Do you know I am not sure I will fully love again?

Today, I hope that I will. Though yesterday, I had not cared at all.

Today, I have felt I loved you again.

Six

-

Those mother fuckin' cunt! They were fucking with the Dead Bod Man. They thought they come into my bunker, and find me? And take me hostage? Me? No! It is I that catches everyone, and it is I that holds everyone hostage. There was never a time for me to be caught, there was never a place for me to be caught, the only thing that existed was the ultimate reality of my absolute freedom. No one can tell me what to do, no one can ever contain me. No one can ever contain the multitudes of desire within me to fuck and kill and slaughter and mar.

You think you know someone, but no one has ever known me. The utter beautiful blackness of my soul was something no one could ever see. And then I romped and raped all through all of the world. Even now, on TV they don't the darkness of my soul. They will never understand the true and pure evil within me. They will never understand how much I NEED to murder them. How much I need their blood – to fucking have it all over them, to have it all over me, to cum all over, to mix all up with my cum, and last but not least, to fucking drink it!

I made my way on my motorbike until I stopped in front of a nice home, ran inside, and killed everyone inside, raped all their butts and a new one, raped their necks where their heads used to be, and then I jacked all over them. And ate all their bodies. Right now I am in bed jacking and jacking, thinking of the next steps in my plan to fucking Kill Holden, and Fucking kill that fucking Fionae. Then that will be the fucking end of all of it.

14

One

-

What is the next step in the mother fucking plan? I
thought of a few things, but I am so fucking angry at
Holden, I am going to do what I do best, and go kill
that mother fucker FIRST! That is the plan!!!!! Do you
have any idea how many people I have killed? How
many fuck and murders I have planned? This is going
to be exactly like every other, as soon as I Isolated it
as the one thing to do, I knew that!!! It's planned, the
moves are planned just like every other fuckin' one,
over time. They are fucking perfected, after every
fucking one. This is going to the magnum opus of

fucking killing fuckers. Hang on a fucking sec. I gotta

lean over and bang this one out. I have a head here.

I'm gonna get this mouth open here. NOW!!!! I fucking

bang my dick so hard it is bleeding fucking

everywhere, drippin' all over the face, and it's just

around the corner. I scream, "Fionae I'm gonna kill

you in a second!!!" And then I fucking cum all in the

mouth. After I bang the back of its throat, until there is

not one fucking bit of hard on left. Bam, bam, bam,

that is fucking it. It's not much of a mouth any more.

It's all stained fucking blue, inside, out, fucking

everywhere. I grab some of the blood, lick it off my

finger, fucking good.

I grab a little more, sprinkle it all up in the air, then it rains down on me. That's good enough to get in the covers and fuckin' pass out, because I have a busy day tomorrow of doing whatever the fuck I want…

AND KILLING FUCKING HOLDEN!!!!!!!

Two

-

I wake up, hard, and I am so fucking into it, I am just pulling at it, I am still in the covers, and I drag em' around with me. Where was the body? There is the body of the head I was porking. I grab it and right away I turn it around and my dick is in the butt. And I

am giving it the time of a lifetime. And the time of his

lifetime. If it was alive, it would be loving it, right?

Right? Fuck yea, it would be. Okay, so I keep going

here, and then I grab a lamp, break it all over the

mother fucker's spine and back. Glass all rolling down

its back and landing on my dick. And I'm still jacking.

Now I'm bleeding out my dick so hard, it's even

spurting. Almost fucking there. This is fucking sexy. I

think I could shoot the fucking glass. It's spurting so

hard it's gettin' in my eyes as I go… No, wait. I take

the lamp and cut the fuckers back open with it.

There's some bone there and its cutting my dick up,

but I'm fuckin' it as I cum so fucking hard, hard as fuckin' Zeus, all over its insides, in a new hole, and I'm gaspin' for air, I had orgasmed so fucking high and hard. Ah, ah, aghh. What a fucking blast. Rarrrrrrr! All you fucker hear, the Dead Bod Man is the fucker and killer of all time, and the fucker killer of all time one hundred years in the future, still. One million years in the future, he's the fucker and killer of all time, still!!!!!!!!!!

Three

-

In terms of getting ready, I am the absolute best in

the universe. In terms of putting on my fucking back

sweats, my fucking black sweater. And my fuck black

ski mask, I do it more fucking swank and sexy than

anyone in the fucking 212, the 718, the uptown the

downtown, in fucking Arkansas, fucking Mongolia,

better than any mother fucker, any fucking where, in

the entire fucking world.

When I'm all dressed I'm the most successful

Lotharian mega motha-fuckin' murderer of all time

and fucking anything else. Holden... Let's

go!!!!!!!!!!!!!!!!!!!!!!!!

Before I go I pull my fucking pants down, and I'm

cumin all over the phone picture of Holden, smiling,

holding his fucking book. Aghh this is going to be the

best feeling ever!!!!!! I dig my fingernail right into my

arm, and then I drizzle some blood over the picture.

There, that's exactly what you needed. A finishing

touch. A draw a little with blood across his neck.

Dead!!! That's what you are, you're dead, you hear

me! Arghhhhh!

Four

-

I'm on my fucking motor bike now, and I'm fuckin'
rippin right, through the fuckin' streets, like slickest
greasiest murdarah(murderer you know) of all time!!!!!
I'm on my way to pick off Holden, and end the mother
fucker's fuckin' time on earth!!!!

I pull up beside the cunt. I mean I pull beside his
apartment. I decided to fast forward my narration a
little. I'd tell all this to fucking anyone. But I decided to
skip to this part where I'm here, to murder the fucking
cunt!!!!!!!!!

I park the thing, I guess I'll need it to get back home.

OR to wherever is next. Tell you the truth I am not

sure I can go back to the cunt bag place right now

with those fuckers having spotted me out. I'm plannin'

just to take another fucker in another part of town.

Just one fucking house… not one fuck will be on to

me. And so everything is going to go on exactly the

fucking same right after this.

I storm up the stairs. There's not one second I'm

waiting to kill this mother fucker. Little does he know

even now I've copied his fucking key. Borrowed while

he was fucking his miss one time, copied later. Had

the watch the end and blow over the window of

course.

I am right through the fucking door. It's not my way to scream and let them know ahead, but I think about it, I think about going Holden, you're fucking dead!!!!!!!!!

When I come in, I don't hear him and I am all worried. I sniff around, is the fucker even here? I am super worried and I start opening up every room and fucking looking for him.

I check through every room. He might not be here. I check every corner of the fucking apartment. He is not here. At this point am I angry beyond containment. I stop everything and pull at my fucking dick as hard as it can. I never thought of this before, but maybe I'll squeeze it so hard it will burst so bad I can't put it back together. I love my dick, and I don't want that to happen. But that is how angry I am!!!!!!!

I'm tugging and tugging, squeezing as hard as I can. I come uncontrollably all over the apartment floor. But it doesn't burst except a little bit. It's good for future Dead Bod Man adventures. I know he's not there, so I run out of the apartment, while I am pulling my pants up.

I get back on my motorbike and it hurts a fucking lot. It hurts so fucking good, and I ride fucking fast with

my full weight on it feeling the pain. Fuckin' fuck yea
and fuck yea for the Dead Bod Man.

I'm roarin' down the highway to the other side of
town, and pretty soon I'll have my mouth and throat
full of fucking dead brains, and my dick halfway up
someone's backside.

15

One

-

Anger, is the best damn feeling in the world.

There isn't one thing I could fuck up. All of my best work I have done when I'm angry.

But most people think you have to stop at a certain point. Well, the Dead Bod Man says, no, don't stop, keep going!

Go until you won't to hurt absolutely everyone, until
you want to hurt yourself. Until all of your victims are
dead and full of cum in every fucking orifice. Until
every single inch of them is covered in that.

I'm the Dead Bod Man. But who are you? What will
make your fucking mark on the fucking planet where I
fucking live. And where you fucking live…?

The Fucking End.

Two

-

The great dame of this novel is coming around.

Fionae is ready to chase love again. One day she will be in love again. I am sure of it.

She is ready to chase love with me again. And one day she will be fully in love with me again. I am sure of it.

I love her deeply, and I dream of her love returning.

The last time we made love I didn't know any of this would happen. But it's okay. And I will cherish the next time just as much as I cherish that one. The last time I felt completely close to her.

The Dead Bod Man put a distance between us, but the gap will close with our love increasing, until our lips touch and our bodies are one again.

Three

-

One, and two, and three, are those the only steps necessary to getting there?

I have to go to the bathroom. One. And two. And
three.

If I could take make that first move, and then take that
first step,

If I could embark on my feet, to the bathroom.

It would mean everything to me.

There is no one around. It is just me and my

destination. And courage.

I am going to go for it. It hurts so much, but I life

myself up and put my weight on my left side.

It is just as painful to move my leg, but I reach my

right foot to the ground.

It is on the floor. I breathe deep for a moment. Then I put my weight on my foot.

I place my other for on the ground, and I stand up. I support my weight on the bed.

Another deep breath. Then I take my first step. I don't fall over.

Then I take step after step to the bathroom. Each one

is grudgingly slow, and when I make it the bathroom, I

put my hands on the toilet, pull myself down,

Mercifully, I pee.

Four

-

Over the next two weeks, Holden got a little more

acclimated at home, by way of just sleeping there at

night, showering, and having something to eat in the

morning. He ate dinner at the hospital most nights,

and all of his free time, and really all of his time

writing, were spend at the hospital. When he watched

tv, it was just in the waiting room. When he read the news, it was in the waiting room. And when it came time to work, he worked in the waiting room.

His writing had been frustrating to carry out without Fionae being able to live her life fully. She was never able to go an adventure with him, and he found his books were getting more boring? Could he just be getting distracted. Once he found himself writing, and for one hundred pages, no character at all had sex. Was that his life right now? Was that sort of who he was? Well, it was just a temporary thing, Fionae would be fully back to herself in a short time. He was sure she would make a full recovery now, and there was really no way to think otherwise. It was too stressful and too painful. Anyone would prefer never to think of it.

He visited Fionae every morning. The room smelled
of a fresh garden, as many mornings he brought
Fionae flowers from the garden shop on the way into
the hospital. She appreciated them a lot, and she
would have the nurses or a tech water them every
single day. Sometimes she would start things off by
watering the plants within reach of her, and then
handing off the water can to a nurse. They were all
fully healthy, she made sure they got sunlight and
everything, and it kept the room smelling very fresh.
Often, Holden wondered she wasn't feeling a little
funny, being in there with them 24/7. It was hard to
gage whether she was improving rapidly, or whether
she was a little intoxicated by the fumes. Obviously, it
was improvement, but boy, the smell of those flowers.

Five

-

Holden and Fionae's walk approached. Holden
arrived one day, and as he was opening the door, he
stopped and watched for a minute. Fionae had been
out of bed, without alerting anyone. She was testing
her feet, walking slowly to the far side of the room. He
noticed she was beginning to shake a little. Knowing
she was feeling week, he walked in and went over to
support her.

It wasn't a second too soon, as she begging to lose
strength. He saw that her legs were beginning to
buckle, and he ran towards her and held her in his
arms. As he held out his arms to her, she was
beginning to fall to the ground. He held one hand

around her waist, and the other on her shoulder as he supported walking back to her hospital bed.

"Thanks, hun. If it wasn't for you. There, wouldn't be a tomorrow. At least for me," She said.

"I am always here. Now don't do that again," Holden said.

Her improvement was uninterrupted given that Holden was able to save her. Thus her recovery sped along, and day after day of people offering physical and psychological care, and day after day of Holden being there with loving support, Fionae got better, and she approached full health.

Six

-

On the day of the walk itself, Holden got ready with significant excitement. He hoped the walk would go really well, and he dreamed of it going amazing, and of their tender love receiving a resurrection. He dreamed of having her stand up straight, even stand up on her toes, and kiss him upon the bridge, underneath a warm sun, though such things were still just a fantasy, she was not so strong yet.

After he got to the hospital, and after he walked into her room, Fionae had been sitting up, she was now ready to go. It was not going to be as picturesque an adventure as you would think. A nurse had left Fionae's walker by the bed. She would be walking with some assistance. Though the opportunity to go outside, and experience nature, and nice weather, was there.

Holden helped her up out of bed, and supported her until her hands were firmly on the walker, reminiscent of a lawnmower, or one of those triangle sleighs for beginning skaters. Now they walked out of the room, and out of the hospital. They moved slowly, Holden just keeping her pace aside her, as she pushed the cart.

They took the elevator down to the ground floor, and walked out of the building to explore the paths around. She wasn't tiring and she smiled and looked around, happy to be out of the hospital for the first time in months. The sun was shining, it was warm, but not too warm, and there were very few people around to inhibit their privacy.

They made their way through the paths, zig zagging through a few of them, they were small in length. A small creek rustled alongside most of their trajectory.

"This is exactly like I imagined it would be," Fionae said.

"Truly, it couldn't be any better," Holden said.

"Maybe when I can about run we could be you know, on this path, but you'd be, you know, about inside my mouth."

"That would be when you're feeling fully better."

"Yea, that's not now."

They approached the bridge, and Holden gave just a

little bracing so she climbs the mild slope. At the apex of it, they stopped and they leaned against the barrier.

"This is as perfect as I imagined it, this moment," Fionae said.

"I'd been thinking of this moment, too. This is perfect, you're right."

"Well, you know what I want to do now."

They leaned into together for a kiss. Their closed lips met, while she leaned over from her walker, and Holden causally held onto the top of the wood barrier. They held their kiss, until Fionae opened her mouth. He opened his a little, and she shoved her tongue in his mouth, waving it around passionately. It was like the first kiss in a love so strong and so famished, that they were starved for its nourishment. They made out for a minute or two, and then they looked off into the distance.

Afterwards, they walked on along the path. Holden braced her form the other side this time, and as they walked around the loop, back to side they came from, they reached the exit of the paths. They walked out of the woods, and back to the hospital.

They walked inside, took the elevator, and when they reached her room, Fionae took one hand off the walker at time to hug him, and then they parted ways for an hour or so, so she could take a nap.

Seven

-

It didn't take long to figure out where that mother

fucker had been hiding. He's been in that hospital

seeing that cripple Fionae every fucking day since we

last parted. I am going to murder every single particle

in his body. There won't be one left in the world.

There will be no memory of this Holden the person.

They'll think I wrote his damn books! There is not

going to be one measley person on earth that thinks

he was ever fucking alive!!!!

I had broke into a house not very fucking far from the

highway. I murdered the fuckin' misses right near the

front door, then I had her down her knees giving me

suck while I bashed her head with a hammer. All the

blood gushing onto me while she's dead sucking me,

aghh, fucking great. I loved it. If there was a league of

serial killers and we came up with terms, we'd love

the dead fuck just about more than anything. Fuck

yeah.

And to tell you the truth I got the husband on the

stairs, through down all of him, dead, then I stepped

on his spine, which was more than a little injured,

broke it right in half, then I Fucked in every hole that

made in both halves. After I napped up real good,

and. I have been planning how I am going to get this

Holden, and this Fionae, ever since. Although I

wanted to go him right away, can't yet, so nothing to

do but plan. They're fucking dead dead dead!!!!!!!!!!!

Fini

1

There isn't a fucker I can't fuck up.

Did they think they could escape?

Did they feel they would live?

Why the fuck would anyone make it so difficult for

me?

Just fucking lose!!!

Lose for me!!!

Lose for me loves!!!

See, I'm nice actually,

Fuck you you fucking cunts ass wipes awful bad

murder subs I could kill a fucking sex gang right now.

Bahahahaha, hahahahaha , muahhahahaha,

muahahahahahaha.

*

One

-

Fionae recovered in time. Physically, she began walking more and more regularly after her first one with Holden. Mostly just inside the hospital, but nonetheless she walked. She regained mobility most days, and she began to feel sturdier, and more comfortable on her feet, all the time.

After a while, she was starting to walk without the support of the walker. Just very short distances at first. But eventually she could walk throughout the hospital. At a certain point, she could walk around the grounds for fifteen minutes or so. Around this time she was starting to feel more comfortable thinking about what happened. She could talk about some of the things that occurred, and she found it to be cathartic every time, and over time she felt less scarred from her encounter with the Dead Bod Man.

When she didn't have the energy for a walk, she often sat in the garden, coming to terms with everything, trying some silver lining… at least she was alive. At least now she was okay physically. She often thought, emotionally, that can only be around the corner, right?

It didn't occur over night, but two weeks went by where she thought could go home. Then a few days went by when she thought of having sex with Holden again for almost the whole day. She masturbated silently nearly the whole time. And at the point she felt she ready for sex again, she knew she was ready to go home.

So after she told the hospital staff she was feeling okay, and ready to go home, she had an evaluation a day later, and then she was discharged. She planned to have sex with Holden again in exactly three days.

Two

-

Holden was waiting for outside as she was rolled out in a wheelchair. He took her hand, and she happily put her hand in his, and they walked together to his Tesla. He helped her in the passenger seat, and then he got in the drivers' seat, and they off back to their place. This was Holden's as generally they had lived together, though the Dead Bod Man can throw a wrench in a lot of your plans. You find yourself in a whole lot of different places.

They both felt comfortable at Holden's, it was safer than her place was. She still kept it just in case, perhaps even just for convenience. But the important thing was someone being there for Fiona right now. The important thing was her not being alone.

And so staying with Holden once again was no-brainer. If there could be a reward for writer's aside from their work, for just being the best human being, that was Holden. He was the best guy on the planet.

Everything was familiar inside. There has been one issue. "Is the smell gone?" Fionae asked.

"Yes, in fact it was right next to you. And other than that, there was no remanence of him anywhere else. Just a few doors left open."

"Okay. And they saw him outside my apartment, so this a lot safer anyways."

"That's right, he was in it too, he went through all of your things, stole some of your underpants and bras."

"Yes, that's right, and it wasn't very cute at all. It was the worst serial killer of all time."

"For sure it was no first timer, it was a very hardened criminal. The worst serial killer ever, in fact. Of course, of course.

"Alright."

Holden unpacked her suitcase for her, putting her clothes in the second bureau, and after watching him a few second, she had a huge urge to pull his dick out and give him a blow job. Was that sex, well it was better to wait, I guess. But she thought it was a good sign she wanted to have some kind of intercourse already. The more she thought about it, the more she really wanted his dick all in her mouth. She sort of kept her mind from thinking about him fucking her super hard. She could tell she'd be thinking about that by tomorrow.

*

What is love? And why do I feel it again?

Because it is undying. Between me and Holden.

Could you define your love in such a way?

Is it between you and such a person as Holden?

While someone has caused me such suffering, no

such thing will happen because of Holden. I know

that.

And I know he can love me if I will forever be only half

of myself. Emotionally. Because he is going to get all

of me physically, and I'm going to fuck until I feel

better.

*

Three

-

The next day, they prepared to spend most of the day
inside. Fionae was just adjusting slowly. After
breakfast, she sat down on the couch, and asked
Holden to sit with her. She wanted to make out, and
they had for ten minutes, getting very reacquainted
with each other. Fionae wanted to bang very badly,

just like she thought. By now, she liked imagining herself bouncing up and down on top of him, and she wanted it badly. She thought she could wait a couple more days though, and when they were done making out, she was around reading while Holden worked on a new book.

He typed quietly while she lay around, not really getting up, and yawning occasionally. In fact she fell asleep around three pm, and napped all the way until dinner.

They ate at the dining table, when they had roasted chicken, baked potatoes, a variety of vegetables. They dug into several wines, and they talked somewhat amusedly about art and literature and politics.

Four

-

The next day Fionae felt a little better still, and she had a similar day, reading lots. Instead of a nap, she went on a long walk accompanied by Holden, through the neighborhood streets.

In the nighttime, after dinner, she lay on Holden's shoulder, more his arm, and they watched movies they hadn't seen yet from the collection on Netflix.

Five

-

Then on the day after that, Fionae had been feeling a lot better. After breakfast, Holden was just rinsing off the dirty dishes. She got up from the breakfast table, and walked over to the sink. She got down on her knees, unzipped him, and pulled his dick out. She started sucking just like she'd given a blow job yesterday. She wanted a fuck bad, and it had been on her mind all morning. She thought of how hard she wanted him to bang her, and she sucked just like that.

She motioned for him to get up on the counter, and once he was on it, she jumped on his dick, and started fucking a little more slowly at first. Eventually she was fucking him super hard.

This was it, exactly the fucking thing she wanted, the thing she had dreamed about the last few weeks, the last month. She knew she was going to come by halfway through, and it just made her fuck harder. Holden handled it find, and she liked knowing her boyfriend was tough. She thought maybe one time she would even like to fuck so hard they would be one step away from the Dead Bod Man's pace. She didn't want to rip him up at all, he didn't want to rip her up at all, but what if they just stopped right before that.

She closed her eyes and sunk his dick into her cunt while she fucking came. It happened a few times. And then she grabbed the sink hose, climbed off him, and ran the water down his stomach. She sucked his dick as hard as she could, while the water ran down onto it, it was the moistest feeling you could imagine, and there was never a louder sound of a blow job ever, she gurgled the water while she fit the whole cock in her mouth, and he came into it, while she had it all shoved in.

She let it out and then said fuck yeah. Semen oozed out her lips, and she took a finger, lipped it up, and swallowed every last drop of his cum. She wanted one last thing, and so she held him in her arms for a tight hug, while her breathing returned to normal, and meanwhile she thought well this is life, this is sex.

*

What can come between love?

When do I lose my love?

To death, to separation… will the Dead Bod Man
sever her heart from her.

As she assures me that her heart is mine only, that I
own it. Will she beat on without her heart?

If I can save her from the Dead Bod Man now, then
maybe I can save her for forever.

*

Six

-

After that, she sat having a coffee with him, her hand cupped over his. It was warm, hot almost, even though she filled half with milk. A few things ran through her mind about the last few months. Mostly things about the last couple weeks. Walking back and forth in the room, cramps in her legs. Trying to get her motivation back. Trying to want to have fun.

Some of her thoughts swirled to the Dead Bod Man. It was all terribly unpleasant, and she tried to block out, like she knew was the best option. There was no way to heal from it, while she was experiencing this moment.

She drank the last drops of the coffee. That, combined with the sex, made her feel very awake. She pushed aside, and pulled herself onto the table.

She pushed forward some. She rested her stomach on the table, leaned forward. She tugged his pants down a little, and plunged her face right into his dick. She held the edges of the table as she moved up and down, giving him head.

She gripped the table tightly, and took big dives at his dick, landing the whole thing in her mouth, and throat, like she was fucking it.

She spit it out, her saliva spilling everywhere. She took him for another round, twirling her head to give him the sensation of it sideways.

After she told him to life up the coffee cups. She told
him to get on top of her. She grabbed his penis from
behind her, and guided it into her ass. He places his
hands the sides of the table, and almost laying on top
of her, he started fucking her.

The first time they had anal since her recovery was
going to go slower right? He paced himself, and each
heave she seemed to feel deeply, each one visibly
almost sent an orgasm through her.

She seemed comfortable. She lifted her arms up in
the air, and put her arms around his biceps. "Harder,"
she said.

He started fucking her harder. Her butt squished
while cum oozed from her pussy onto the table.

"Harder," she said. He fucker her a little harder.

"Right now," she said. "Destroy me."

He thought if she seemed ready, then they have sex, really have sex, right now. "Okay," he said. He fucked her hard, almost as hard as when they usually get hardcore. And she moaned and pleasantly screamed exactly like a woman getting the hot sex she wants.

He moved his hands, and pulled away from her some, because he wanted to cum. But she just said, "stay with me, no." Then she said, "Cum right in my ass."

He started moving faster again, up to the same pace, going deep to really make him cum.

Another minute, and he was definitely ready to blow.

He let out a moan, and she spread her legs a little more, so he go blow right in her, and he couldn't hold it anymore, he let it fly, up her ass, into her rectum, and he slowed down to rest as the last bit of his cum dripped into her asshole.

Seven

-

They put their dirty dishes in the dishwasher, and headed for the bathtub. They filled it up, soaking themselves as soon as it was half fill, they soaked in it. When it was full, Holden turned it off. Fiona had been laying in his lap over top of him. She turned over and dunked herself in the water, submerging all her hair, and then she brought her head out, and flicked the water from her hair. She submerged her head again, and put Holden's flaccid penis in her mouth. She warmed it up with good fellatio, and then she brought her head and took a few breaths. Then she went to work, sucking it powerfully, with her head full submerged. Every ten seconds or so, she brings her head up, catches her breath, and then does some more. She did it for ten minutes, then she got on her knees in the bathtub, and put her ass up in the air. She wanted Holden in the cunt.

This time she was even more ready, "Pound me as hard as you can, babe," she said.

He fucked her heard, about as hard as he could. She splashed some water up, so I smacked loudly in the air, between her ass, and his pelvis.

"Give it to me, give it to me," she said.

They fucked like that for another ten minutes, almost eleven minutes. Then she motioned for him to grab her ankles. He held her upside down and she had one hand on the bottom of the tub, one of the edge of it. Her head was under water, while she arched her pussy towards his dick, and he inserted it, and started fucking just as hard.

When she needed a breath, she'd lift her head up to the side, breathed deeply, and then put it down for more.

Sometimes she'd scream passionately, almost for effect, the muffled sound vibrating through the water.

At a certain point, she said, I'm going to cum! And he could barely understand what she said.

He was pretty sure she heard what he said, but he didn't really prepare in anyway, and when she came, it landed on his stomach, thick cum, shooting in a wide arc.

She motioned for him to put her down, and she got on her knees, sucked his penis hard. And when she thought she was ready to come she asked him if he was. He said yea, and she closed her eyes and put her forehead right in front of his dick. He jacked his penis hard, and he came right onto her forehead. It oozed down, past her eyes, onto her lips and mouth, on to her chin. She licked some in, then she threw hair down, got the cum all over her hair, waving it around on her face. Then she took a strand, and sucked all the cum off. Then she did that with another five, six strands. Then she ate all her cum off Holden's chest, and licked every bit of his left on his dick, and then they flipped the drain on.

The water drained quickly, and then they turned the shower on, and showered together, before they toweled off and put new clothes on.

Eight

-

They relaxed together, and Fionae watched the news as Holden wrote some notes for his novel, and watched a little. Fionae needed to rest to recover of course, though basically they thought they'd do that now, as they need to go pick up some new things for her, like new towels, some new makeup, some new books. Novels would keep her occupied while she sat around and recovered.

They would also need groceries. Some more things that she liked, something for dinner. Obviously you can't leave enough for two people around in the fridge, when just one person is eating, it would go bad.

She felt he had typed a lot of notes. It seemed to be more than a page. At the same time, the tv program was not quite over. It was a fairly impressive pace.

Meanwhile she was sure he was thinking of her as well, thinking about whether she felt one hundred precent okay physically, and emotionally as well. She had right now. She was not very interested in the news now. The last segments were not very interesting.

She looked at Holden, though he didn't move his

eyes from his notes. She thought she'd really tried to grab his attention. Lightly, she grabbed his dick. He stopped typing. As she stroked it broadly, he looked at her. She nodded a couple times, miming gimme, and she got on top of him, helped him unzip himself and get his pants off, and then she sunk him in and started humping him.

She rode him with her clothes on for a while. Then she pulled her shirt off, over her head. She puts his hands on her tits, while she unzipped her pants, still riding him. She slid them off without moving much, an then she pulled her g-string up and massaged her clit while she fucked him.

She told him grab the remote and turn it on really loud, there were sound of a Middle Eastern conflict, sound of politicians having news conferences, sports highlights being quickly covered.

Once the volume was higher, she relaxed, and really went at him. She bounced right on his organs, knowing he'd be okay. To be honest he'd be a little sore.

She had another coffee, and she took a sit, then moved down to his dick, and sucked it. He could feel the heat of it, and she sucked it super quick. She took another drink of it, a little bit of oozing down his dick the next she sucked, and the pain was almost simmering hot, especially as her lips first touched his penis.

She did this for a while, and he felt the pleasure of it. Then she got ready to ride him again. First, she took his pants off, and his boxers, and his shirt. Then she grabbed the coffee, and poured it on his dick. She waited a minute for it to cool, and then she hopped on, using the coffee as a lubricant.

She fucked as hard as she could, moaning again. "Fuck yea," she screamed.

After a couple minutes, she slipped in the ass, and this time not holding back at all, she fucked as hard as she could, before she threw him right back in the front, coffee oozing out her pussy, and down his dick at this point.

She kept doing that for a while, then got up and sat on the coffee table. She bent over, and she grabbed the remote. She took both batteries out, and shoved them both in her pussy. She inserted Holden right into her ass, and she poured a little more coffee over his dick with her other hand. She massaged herself with batteries while they were having anal sex.

They fucked like that for a good ten minutes, then she grabbed a black blanket of the couch, and put it over her face. "Cum all over me like I'm the Dead Bod Man," she said.

He jacked off, until he came, all over the blanket pulled around her mouth and nose, and then she turned it around, wiped it all over her mouth, and then drank down all the cum.

She leaned over to him, and kissed his chest twice,

then she got up and went to the sink.

*

WHO the fuck do they think they are!!!!!!!!!!!!!!!!!!!!!!!!

Well, it is only a matter of time. I capture everyone.

And while I wait, I think about it? Do they deserve at

all to, not be captured?

Sometimes I decide, they do.

BUT, it does not matter. The Dead Bod Man must kill.

It is what he does. What we need to kill we must

capture.

What I thought I would kill I was right to kill, and thus I

will. I damn will, and that will be the end of it.

Did they deserve another direction... of life? No. This is one of history, and it is the one history is going to take.

*

Nine

-

They went out for dinner, as Fionae was anxious to do something out of a sitting environment. They chose a restaurant they go to often that serves Japanese food. Afterwards, there is a spot they know, a nightly rental apartment, that sets above an aquarium. Beneath the floor of the apartment is the Killer Orca's tank. Six of them swim around, that you can see through the glass floor. It is several layers thick, finished so that you can't break through it.

They took the blankets off the bed, and lay them atop the tank. Fionae lay on her back above the blankets, and Holden ate her out, while they could smell the aquatic elements of the tank, and they could smell the flesh, and excrements of the Orca's.

At a certain point Fionae turned around, and made a triangle with her body, and he banged her that way, with no reason to think he'd break the glass floor.

Afterwards, Fionae held built-in bar stool, as Holden held in the air a little, and still banged her. She could see the Orca's swimming around in the tank directly beneath her, and she felt flayed a live, she felt strung just above them.

They were ready to come so she turned over, and he shot in her face, with just the tank behind her head. Then Holden went down on her as she came up in the air. And afterwards, he grabbed the blankets, and they lay back in the bed, falling asleep.

Ten

-

The next morning, they drove home, and pulled into the parking garage around 9 30. Holden held Fionae's hand as they climbed the hill in the parking garage to the elevator, and all the way up to the room. They got off on their floor. Holden inserted the key into the door, and swung it open.

And then it happened. He had been standing right there, in the dark, in their apartment. And all of the sudden, two darts hit them. He shot one dart at Holden, and one dart at Fionae. And they both went down in second. The Dead Bod Man had done it again. They were both recaptured. And they were captured together now.

2

One

-

Who is the Dead Bod Man? He's the mother fuckin' baddest baddy on the whole fucking Earth. Ain't no one badder anywhere. There's no gang even that reeks as much fuckin' havoc as me. I'm the baddest of the baddest killa's there ever fucking was.

And who the fuck gets off? Who the fuck gets off one hundred times each and every day. The mother fuckin' Dead Bod Man, just me, and not anyone else on the entire fuckin' earth. You might not have noticed, but it's every mother fuckin' day I'm getting' off inside of a bod. Sometimes it's a dead bod. Sometimes, at first it's a live bod. Then after it's afuckin' dead bod that I'm mother fuckin cranked at least thirty times, maybe three thousand. Fuckin' cunt, all the Dead Bods out there that don't know it. They're fuckin' soon to be.

So if you weren't aware of the Dad Bod Man, you've been made aware. No one fucks with me, no fucks better than me, and no one fucks more than me. Have you heard of an opinion. Well forget about those, because I only give you the fuckin' facts.

You think I hadn't captured those mother fuckers? You think some fucker hadn't told you about it already?

I'm sure this book we're puttin' together for you made that clear. Well I fuckin' caught the fuckers. Like the most pro fuckin' predator of all time. Better than a

Cheetah, better than a Lion, better Cougar, just straight fuckin' gangster, and straight fuckin' deadly as mother fuckin' fuck. Fuckin fuck yeah.

So I captured, and are they hanging off a cooking stick, over a fire. No, not right now. Not yet. There fuckin sittin' down there. In my fuckin' bunker, just fuckin' lovin' every fuckin' second. Of my fuckin' torture. There just fuckin' havin' the time of their lives. Their just getting fuckin' mutiliated. Their getting' fuckin' destroyed. Ain't nothin' nobody can do about either. Have you noticed a fuckin' interlude? Had you? Had you fuckin' noticed that.

I had to build a WHOLE new bunker some other mother fuckin' place. You think I'll tell you where it is but I am not even fuckin' gonna drop a single hint in any way whasofuckin'ever. I'll tell you where they fuckin' are, you don't get to know where they fuckin' are, that's where they fuckin' are. But readers it's not you I mean to insult, keep on fuckin' readin'. But please jack! And jack and jack and jack. I know you had, because my shit is so fuckin' hot. You'd not see it comin' when you picked this book up, but I filed it with so much hot shit, all the dames and all the dudes will be jackin' for centuries. And don't you ever fuckin' say I told you where they are, I not fuckin' had.

Now I'm watchin' em. I got a fuckin' glass wall, really tinted. Of course it is one fuckin' way even it's one of those. In fact this seems to be my new favorite hobby, I'm even loosen' interest in other hobbies. I just fuckin' sit there and I'm fuckin' twerking as fuckin' hard as I fuckin' can, peerin' through the fuckin one side glass. Just for fuckin' hours they can't tell I'm watchin'. They're talkin' and talkin' like I can't hear, and I'm just losin' my shit on my dick. And when they're gone to the bathroom I have to force myself to keep my eyes open, cause I'm fuckin' lovin' every fuckin' second of it to the point where I'm nearly in a dream. But I keep watchin' every second to make sure I don't miss even one thing.

I think I might have jacked for twenty-four hours straight. Did you know I write that fuckin' slow? I barely had a second to even update this story I'm writin' for yea! Oh fuck yea, Oh my god. Are you getting in on this? Oh my fucking god.

Two

-

Now I'm getting really pissed off. I'm going to have to leave my jackin', to do my second favorite hobby. Can you BELIEVE these fuckers. They're going to make me leave my hobby for my second favorite hobby. So that's kickin' the crud out of them, and torturing them, so that's what I'm going to go do now. These mother fuckers are the worst kind of fucker they're ever was, making me go to do my second favorite hobby. Unbelievable.

I unlock the gate. Slam it closed, locked it again. I walk right up to them, livid, absolutely pissed off, and I put on my spiked knuckles. And the first thing I do I slam that stupid Fionae across the fuckn' face with em'. I just felt die fuckin' a-hole! Then I unzip her onesie that I've made her wear every day for weeks and she'll surely wear till' she dies, and I just beat her pussy with the knuckles. Fuckin' bam, bam, bam, one after the other. And she screams so fuckin' loud every mother' fuckin time. Every mother fuckin' thrust. Every one she gives the howl of a fuckin' lifetime. The mother' fuckin' a-hole. Then I just stick my dick right in. Fits like a glove right around the rushin' blood. And I just fuck her guts out. Not literally yet, but some of them are flyin' in the air as I bang her. And meanwhile she's still screamin' now. She's like ahhhhhhh. And no one can fuckin' her hear way down her, way way underground in my new layer, which is in the middle of fuckin' nowhere anyways. Fuckin' lady. Sex God of the past, no one can fuckin' hear you!!!!!!!!!!!!

Three

-

You think I'm fuckin' done there? Then I fuckin' slap her upside the side of the face. I garb a chair and fuckin' brake it over her body like a wrestler but for fuckin' real. If you were looking for not a faker, then that was me, and that fuckin' person you've been fuckin' looking for. If you didn't know it, it was I, the fuckin' Dead Bod Man.

Your boy. All this shit I did. No worries. No fuckin' worries whatsoever. So I wasn't done. I did have somethin' planned a little more than fuckin and fuckery. I take my fuckin' lighter out and I pull her leg up and hold it the in the air.

'Who do you love,' I ask her.

'Holden,' she says.

'Ya,' I say. Then I fuckin' light her whole foot on fire.

'Noooo!' She screams.

'Tell me who you love.'

'I love… I love the Dead Bod Man.'

'What did you just say to me?' And I add more fuel to the fire.

'I love the Dead Bod Man!'

'Good,' I say. But I let it burn a little more, the way it is. I count to ten. A little slower than normal time. Then I take my handkerchief and haphazardly smother it out. I still got her mother fuckin' hands tied up, and I leave it smoldering a little. And I drop her leg.

She's fuckin' tryin' to rub it along the dirt. Suppose
that work a bit. Whatever. I'm fuckin' out there. I gotta
get the jack out of me before the pleasure of all a this
is gone.

*

You think I'm fucking JOKING that I need to jack every fucking second!!! I not fucking joking!!!

EVERY FUCKING SECOND not lived in ecstasy is a fucking waste. Oh my fucking GOD!!!!!!!!!!!!!!

What a fucking waste normal life is!!!!! If I have to feel like a normal fucker even one second I am going to off those fuckers right now!!!!!!

*

Four

-

I have never felt so much pain in my entire life. That monster, who I would never confuse for a man, lit my right foot on fire. Oh my god. My foot is obviously going to be burned for the rest of my life. What amount of surgery could possibly fix it.

Is it okay? Am I going to be able to walk on this? Right now I can't be totally sure, but like, probably. It seems okay. The shape is there. I could feel my skin melting in the flame, but the tissue inside it felt only warm. Sure it was hot on the edges. But I knew if it didn't go on much longer I'd still have my foots.

I'd like Holden's opinion, but he's tied up right now. So in my opinion it's going to be alright, and I sure hope Holden can have sex in socks.

The flames are almost gone now. I place my bottom of my foot on the ground. How does it feel? It honestly hurts a lot. But the pain did not go right through my foot. I think I am still walking in the future.

I look at Holden. We lock eyes. He begins to cry. I have to cry as well. Suddenly tears are running down my face, and they are running down his as well.

The inability to do anything is agonizing. I close my eyes and I think of Holden eating my pussy. It makes me feel the pain a little less. 'Holden, I want you to eat me, the first chance you get, okay.'

'Okay,' he says.

"And not like the dead bod man, you know.'

'Yea, I knew, I knew what you meant.'

'Good, good.' I say. 'Holden, you can still fuck me can't you?'

'Yea, that foots going to be fine. I think surgery can fix a third of that burn for sure.'

'For sure, and what are socks for?'

'I'll fuck you with your sucks on. Fine. And I'll fuck you with them off.'

'Then you'll always be my guy.' I said. 'And Holden."

'Yea?'

'Let's get out of here in one piece.'

'Done. Let's make it happen.'

There was noise coming from another room. Just like one over. It was the loudest beating I'd ever heard. It was in the other room, but...

'Is he doing what I think he's going?' I ask.

'He's crazier than we thought.'

'Oh my god.'

'He's so sick.'

'I know.' I say. 'Honey, he's watching us.'

'There's glass there.'

'It must be one way.'

'Then he's watching.'

'Now we know. There's some way out of this.'

'Yea. No. Maybe.'

'Just believe me.'

'Alright.'

Five

-

Do you suffer from mother fucking excessive stress? I know you fuckers do. Well look no further than myself, I can show not just how to have no stress, but fuckin' negative stress. Like ahhhhhhhh. Do you have a Dead Bod?

I didn't think so. No one is as good as me. Maybe get at good at gettin' one of those of your own. Me I got one all the time. And twenty in stow. I'm grabbin' it and going to town on it's a-hole. If you experience any blueness of the dick, that's nothin', and just keep going. Don't ever fuckin' think twice about that. You fuckin' hear?

Don't mother fuckin' ever think twice about that shit. Now I grabbin it's arms and pulli' em so hard there's almost tearin off. Ain't holdin' nothin else while I pound its ass. Got a nifty one, I do sometime. Slit its chest, and now I fuckin it's heart. My dicks goin' boom, boom against it's hear. And I'm gonna cum.

I drop a load all over the dead chick's heart. Oh my fucking god, nothing would complete you, could compelte, more in the earth, in the stars, in the universe. Oh my fuck… Aghggh. Just emptyin' it like cortisol all over the walls of that fucker. Ughh heart, take that. Ugghh.

How could you cum on a person's soul? I'd say it's a bit like that. You just get it all over their heart. And if they WERE alive, you're cum would be going all through essence, all through being and soul, they be fucked so good, you about own them. Like God, making proper Christians of them all and your Christ.

Where are those fuckers. I bound out. And I burst into their chamber. I march up to Fionae, and I am so fucking livid. I am going to take this one's heart for a cum, even if it means killing it before I have hardly even played with it.

I lean down and hold her by her throat. 'Give me one

good reason why I shouldn't cut your heart out right now?'

She gives me no response.

'Huh? Would you die? You would die. Is that a reason?'

'Yes,' she replies.

'Alright. That is a reason.' What I want right now is to cum on a live heart. I don't think anything can stop me.

'Alright I won't cut it out. But I'm going to perform an open heart. Sometimes they die during these. So just bear with me.'

'No," she complained.

'Shut your mouth. I'm fuckin' doing it.'

I ready myself to make the cut. I mean I would love nothing more than to get to toy with my prey for a couple months here. I mean I have been planning it since the second they got here. That'd be a lot of thought lost if nothing came of this.

So I'm ready to go. And I hover the knife right above the sternum. Then I fuckin cut. And she's screamin, being cut open alive, having everything around her heart carved and such.

I am freakin' jokin that I care a lot, and I am cutting it up like fuckin speed art. Boom, bada big, bada boom. Hmm. Hehmmmmm. Hmm. Hehmmmmm. Like fuckin' music. Oh my fuckin' god it's the best fuckin' stuff.

Almost there, got a lot of the bone cleared. I can't

fuckin' stand the end. That's when you might screw up abit, plus you've been workin' so fuckin long. The beginning, when you dig it deep, and just fuckin' let the blood gush everywhere, that is fuckin' parfait. Aggh, finger lickin' good. But… when that heart is finally ready for a little watering, oh man, that's the fuckin' best.

So this part is like right before the finish line in some marathon, and then I get that finished, cum ready opening, just like crossing the finish line. I think it's fuckin' ready, I step back, admire my work about. And voilà, I have never seen something so ready for the cum department to cum along and fill it up.

I toss the cutting tool up in the air and I grab my dig, and I'm off to work on part deux. Oh fuck yea. Oh my fucking god.

I need a little more of a warm up. I've got Holden tied, so I walk over to him, and flip him over. Don't fuckin' move I tell him. And I pin him and put my dick deep in his ass, and start pounding the fuck out of him.

'You think this is some fucking game?' Holden doesn't answer. But I grab his neck and choke him really hard while I'm doing this, like I'm fuckin' jokin but not really. His head turnin' a little purple, as I'm startin' to feel the pleasure of the cum, it's just like thirty second off now.

I grab his head now, and slam it on the fuckin ground, and I'm sure I fractured his skull just a little. He doesn't pass out, but he's fuckin' dazed. And I fuck his ass as hard as I can. Fifteen seconds left, and I get out of the ass, and I walk back to Fionae, and I start jackin' right above my cum whole. I have never jacked so fuckin' fast. Wait for it, wait for it, and bam!!!!! I cum. And I Cum all in her fuckin' chest, and every fuckin' bit lands right on her hand. And I own this fuckin' woman's soul while she fuckin' lives. Don't mess what the Dead Bod Man. Fuck yea.

That's fucking right. Oh my god. And I can see it, white puddles, bouncin' up and down on top of her scared heart. She be pumpin' my semen 'stead of her blood for fuckin' eons to come. Ain't nobdy ever been as good as nothing as the Dead Bod Man. I close the chest up a bit, then I leave her lying there, and I got back to my chamber to fuckin wack my brains out, most about all the shit that just what down. Fuckin' fuck yea.

Six

-

On to part goo. I know you want to fuckin' hear it. Oh my god, I am wacking so fuckin' hard. Uggh. Uggh. I am tuggin' so hard, bloods flyin' everywhere so hard, there's even some on the ceiling.

Aggghhh. And where am I going to land this, one, on the fuckin' ceiling. Oh my god, every time I think of cumin' on that woman's heart for the rest of my life, I'm going to have to stop and blow one out, and all over some strangers face after I beat them up and threw them on the ground, or on a Dead Bod. Oh my GOD. Ahghahghahgh. Yes.

YES. YES. COME ON. COME ON.

I've got something in the fridge. It's Holden's foreskin. I cut it off while he was awake. I take it out and I'm jackin' full out in every way. And I fuckin' burst on his foreskin, all over it. And that thing is going to be cracklin' with my cum for centuries while I have in this fridge or that fridge. Fuck yea. Take that you stupid fucker. That was not bad. But I can't fuckin' wait for tomorrow. In fact they better something, anything at all, because that's all it is going to take for me move the schedule fuckin' ahead, and just about fuckin' kill em' and fuck em'.

*

THIS is IT!!! I am going in there right this second
to fucking kill them!!! I don't fucking care
anymore!!! I want fucking DEAD BOD sex right
now!!!!!!! I can't stand what he is up to at all!!!!!!

I can't stand what she is up to at all!!! I think it
might be fucking ready right now!!!! Jesus Christ
this require more discipline than being fucking
GOD. I am GOD's GOD, I believe. WELL of course
I am. I am!!!!!!!!!!

*

Seven

-

Lucky for them, they were quite most of the night. I decided to leave them alone for a bit. No one interrupted my divine jacking, and I almost considered just letting them live another day, because that's what this was, something so rough they might die. I was playing with letting them live last night, then this night, I was just playing with them, was there really even any difference? There wasn't. Anyways, now there dead.

I knew what I needed to do when I went in there, and I met them with a cauterizing iron, and two lemons. 'Good day, shit head, and shit head,' I said to them.

'You ready for your greatest test yet?'

'Test? You're just torturing us!' Holden yelled.

'Well, that is true. But all torture is a test of toughness. You don't know who you are, until you have been through horrible torture.'

'So what have I prepared for you today? You may ask this. The answer is the ultimate test of all time. I am not going to cauterize your chest, or your cheek. If you guessed am I going to cauterize, I am. I am going to cauterize your rectum!!!!'

'You can't do that! Anyone would die from the pain.'

'Hmm. Well, funny you should ask, because I would know. Some die, some will live. It depends on the toughness of the test subject. The weak will die, the strong will live. So, prepare to discover whether you deserve to be a member of the human race. Though, in the end, I will kill you.'

'All of you serial killers are the same. It's all about you, then you kill them!'

'Well, yes. Yes, and no. Serial killer? I surely am. But I am a pleasure master. And I am the greatest at both of all time!'

No response. Then I said, 'Well, who's first? I guess I'll decide. You mother fuckers!!!!!! Hmm. Ah. Holden, yes, you first. Come here. Oh wait, you're tied up. I'll come to you.'

I marched over to the fucker, and I kicked him over onto his back. Then I started lighting the iron with my match.

'Oh, you fuckers are gonna get it.'

It wasn't ready right away. Five minutes of lighting the fucker, I aimed it, and then stuck it right up Holden's ass. What made the fucker think I wasn't going to break his anus? I told him he'll probably die. I hod it there a full minute.

Then I take it out, his shit spilling out of his rectum everywhere. And I fuckin love that shit. So I jam my dick in, and poo flying everywhere, I fuck the shit out of him once again. I fucking destroy his asshole. All the poo, all the heat, everything. Just fucking destroying… everything.

Eight

-

Next it's time for that other asshole Fionae. 'Well, one lover, then the other,' I say.

I have some poo on me, it's pretty much all over my dick, flecked with big bits of blood. There's some on my hand but whatever.

'So how's Holden doing?'

She didn't answer right at first. 'Oh you'd better fuckin' answer. It'd be a lot better if you fuckin' answered. Are you gonna fuckin' answer for me?'

'Yes, he's okay.'

'Well, that's a stretch. I destroyed that fucker real

good. But he's alive. That's for sure.' I looked at her, looking to see if she was scared. She didn't look scared enough. That was going to change. 'Now. Time for your fuckin' turn. And you my dear, have a much better chance of dying. You could say, it's your fuckin' year.'

I use the hot iron, and turn her over. I press her back all the way to the ground with it. And then I start sizing up the hole, and planning the procedure.

'Well I'll get my mudfuck. Don't you worry. I need that to be perfect. But whether you live, that's up to some god out there!'

I plunge it it, and bam, this one ruptures in a second. She'd really had to use the bathroom, poo from this beautiful creature flew up all the way to my face. I lick some off with my tongue. Then I take the iron and swing at her mid-section. 'Whaam!!!' I scream.

'What's the use of use other than fucking!!!! The true use of a woman is just to take it, and then die!!!!!'

While she was bleeding and dying was the perfect opportunity for some fellatio. I lean over in that fucking awful beautiful creature's face, and I yell, 'Suck my fucking cockkkk!!!!!'

My dick's always handy and out around the bunker. And she does it. She's suckin' it. And I've trained her up at this point so that when she's suckin' it, she sucks like she likes it, and makes it real good. It's the best fellatio of all time because she fuckin' hates me, but she's suckin' it so good!!!

'Is it like I fuckin' paid you, huh!!!! Tell me you fucking

love me!!!!!!'

'I love you, sir Dead Bod Man.'

'That's more like it.' I roar with excitement.

That goes on for fifteen minutes or so. Then I reckon it's time I get my mud fuck, or it's not going to be really prime.

'Now's the time for cooking the hen honey.'

She stops suckin', and shaking, she turns around and presents her but to me. And I fuck away like nothing had ever been more religious than it, it was an experience of being God and lookin' down everyone itself.'

'Oh my God,' I scream. 'Oh my goddd!!!!!! You, I want to hear you say it to!!!!'

She goes, 'Oh my god. Oh my god. Fuck yea.'

Her voice really quiver on the fuck yea cuz she's
bleedin' and probably feeling pain like hell. And I
fuckin' like it. That's exactly what I fuckin' want, and
by now I cum and I am just gonna keep fucking until I
cum again another five times. Maybe she'll still live.
But long live the Dead Bod Man.

Nine

-

After her butt is a mess with poop and blood
everywhere, blood still gushing out of her rectum.
Blood and poop everywhere on the floor. Typical.
Successful. Succulent. Fuck ya.

'Now give it to me dirty! Oh wait, you had!!!'

Now that's what I am talking about it. We fucked like we were in love. 'It's not that hard to fuckin' take it from the Dead Bod Man. We're ten times closer than we ever were!!!!' And then I left her there, just fuckin dying. No need to even tie em' back up. I'll give em' freedom of that, see if they jack, and see if they feel a bit better. Really I don't care, it's just an experiment.

I head back to my layer, and I know you want to hear about it, oh my god, I jacked so good. There was fuckin' semen all over the control panels, all over the window as I watched both those idiots bleedin' out. It was the best of the best stuff.

3

One

-

Fionae and Holden sat in the chamber with little to no hope for escape. They faced certain death, right around the corner. The only thing that mattered was making sense of their life, figuring out what it meant.

Fionae was bleeding horribly, and Holden, also bleeding, woke from unconsciousness after a few hours, and shortly thereafter found the awareness to go assist Fionae.

He held her in his arms. Perhaps between the two of them, they could find the true meaning of their lives, that they were together, and that their love was beautiful.

The Dead Bod Man had left their clothes around. He grabbed her sweater and quickly started covering the wound to slow the bleeding. He could feel the blood clotting more and more, and the wound closed slowly.

She was bleeding very badly, but he assumed she'd survive. But there was definitely a chance she wouldn't make it. She would probably bleed a least a little for the next few days. She wouldn't be able to move much, otherwise it would gush out. That was the best he could do in the circumstances, to just make the situation better.

She held her eyes open most of the time, so she could look at him, and feel connected as he helped her stay alive. As the bleeding eased, she felt more conscious, and she reached up with her neck, to kiss him, and they kissed lightly. She had poop on her mouth, but she hadn't seemed to notice. He didn't mind. He loved the acknowledgment and the emotion from her.

A few hours later, he figured the bleeding had stopped sufficiently, so he stopped covering the bleeding wound, and lay beside her. She put her arms around him and let her bodies slow healing mechanisms work.

Two

-

Fionae bled slowly for several more days. There was no way to scab the wounds over. She would have needed stitches. So it bled on. At the same time he held her tightly, thinking every bit of love, and soothing could matter deeply. At one point hey had wiped the poop off of each other. When their hands were hands were full completely of each other's poop, they licked their hands of it, eating each other's poop, until they were clean again, and they continue rinsing each other's bodies.

After a day of it being stopped, they were still in a place of pain, and deep traumatization. But Fionae knew from her previous kidnapping by the Dead Bod Man, that she needed to get over it, and try to live life as much as possible.

Her wounds were very tender, so she threw Holden down into her cunt. And he ate her out while she stayed very still. She moaned softly, hoping the Dead Bod Man wouldn't hear.

Her pussy started oozing, and a minute later cum came gushing out, and Holden ate some, thinking that it actually might even keep him alive a little.

He swallowed most of it, then went back to resting his head on her shoulder. And right at that moment, the Dead Bod Man came back in.

Three

-

Hello mother fuckers! Had you fucking survived! Oh my God, there fucking moving, and breathing. What the fucking FUCK!!! Hahahahahahaha!!!!

Come and titty fuck the Dead Bod Man babe. Actually, I got something better for you. How about a sandwich? Because your both so fucking hungry huh!!!! A fucking cum sandwich!!!! From the Dead Bod Man!!! That you should be so lucky, and that you should fucking fucking mother fucking have fucking anything to eat!!!

And wait a second!!! You mother fucker!!! Did you just eat that fucking whore's cum!!! Hah!!! What. The. Fuck. Did you just do.

I walked over there, and I leant over and I licked every fucking bit of cum out of that woman's cunt. Then I fucking chomped on it, taking with me a fucking slice forever of that woman's camel toe.

Then I went and shoved my finger so fucking far down that fucking dude's throat, that he fucking puked almost instantly.

Did you think you'd get any fucking sustenance? Huh!!! What the fucking fuck is wrong with you. Jesus fucking christ, if you don't think I run absolutely every aspect of your life!!!

Fucking fuck you for fucking having that. You don think you're going to eat a guy's cum now too, you fucking are going to!!! About right this second. I spontaneously start jacking. Oh my God. Oh fucking God. This is fucking the best. Now open!!! Open you're mouth!!!

He wasn't really opening it, so I said, fucking open it right fucking now, or I'll fucking kill you. And since I am the Dead Bod Man, of course I will, so he fucking does it. He opens his mouth. And I'm jackin' at the speed of light. And BAM. It's out. It's in his mouth. And I'm rubbin' my dick on his lips. Then I should now close you're fucking mouth. He closes it and I go, now fucking swallow, swallow every fucking last bit.

And he swallows twice. Then I say, now lip you're fucking lips. Lip every fucking inch of your fucking lips!!! Then swallow every fucking bit of it. Swallow every last bit of my cum!!! Swallow it fucking now. Right fucking now!!! Right fucking this second!!!

He swallows it. Ah, alright, I go. Now fucking take this!!! And I kick the fucker in the face. Fucking fuck you!!!

The fucker's bleedin' pretty bad. It's mostly his mouth. What? Do you think I broke your fuckin' mouth. Did I break you're fuckin' teeth. To be honest, I need to know for when you're sucking my dick!!! Open you're mouth.

There good and broken. Good, I say. They're perfect for some rough mouth fucking shit. Some good fucking dick suckin'. That's what I like, to get shit ripped up. Ripped up really fuckin' good.

Suddenly I have something to do so I bounce out the room, and I put the Vagina hood in a fuckin' freezer, the nearest fuckin' one. Of course it's in my viewin' room. Where I'm viewin' them. All the fuckin' time. And that's shit perfectly fuckin' preserved. I'll be jackin' with it for a fuckin' millennia or three.

Four

--

Holden lay there in complete agony. He could feel with his tongue that all of his teeth were still rooted in. He could likely still save most of them, though probably not all of them.

He opened his mouth, to try and move his tongue a little more, so he could get a better sense of the damage, and blood poured out of his mouth. He closed it again, and he felt the blood building against his mouth. He spit some out.

It was quite gross. And Fionae was watching. She was bleeding profusely from the top of her vagina. Sill though, she got up, walked over to Holden, and rubbed his dick. Then she inserted him, and got on him, without smacking his stomach, because of her recently closed wound in her anus. She rode him, enjoying the first time they'd had sex since they were captured. Fuck yea, she said, quiet enough so the Dead Bod Man might not hear.

She was getting ready to cum, and she closed her eyes while her mouth hung open, and she panted, oh, emmm, oh. She came and it splattered on Holden's stomach, along with blood spilling from her Cameltoe area.

A white and red puddle had formed on Holden's chest. Still she fucked him, waiting for her fiancee's first ejaculation in a while.

Fuck yea, she said.

He groaned quietly. Certainly not loud enough for the

Dead Bod Man to hear. He closed his eyes, feeling more pleasure. He was going to come in ten seconds. In five seconds, in three seconds, in two seconds. Bam. And white semen, flecked with brown poop on the end, flew into her vagina. And traveled down into her Uterus.

They lay there afterwards, knowing that inevitably the Dead Bod Man would be back, and that he would know something had happened. They may have been able to deceive themselves for a second, but the excitement gone, the sexual act in the past now, they saw he would know everything. Surely, he would beat them, and beat them senseless.

Five

--

They woke up the next day, and surely it was morning. Though it could have been afternoon. The Dead Bod Man slept and woke up at a normal time right? It seemed he came in right when he woke up.

Today it seemed he wasn't up yet. So Fionae leaned over, opened up Holden's boxers, and gave him his first blow job since their captivity started. She sucked it hard, making sure she didn't swallow literally, keeping all the spit she had in her dehydrated mouth.

She made him feel a little better, and they felt like going on to having sex again. The Dead Bod Man, couldn't hear them, they thought again, and they pushed each towards an orgasm. And feeling a little emotional, enthralled in passion, but okay, they came, and once again his semen crawled up her uterus.

Six

--

It was that mother fuckin' time again!!! The time to go in there and tell those fuckers exactly what's going on. They don't think I caught them!!! Last night!!! And this morning!!!! They don't think I was watching when they started!!! I was just having a loud morning jack in a soundproof room, and then there they are going at it. I mean they are already getting a punishment for last night those fuckers, and then this on top of that, they're getting one HELL of a punishment now. Those fucking cunts. Who the fuck do they think they are, doing that fucking shit, leaving me out, what the fuckin fuck, that is the weirdest fucking shit I have ever fucking heard of. Jesus fucking fucking fuck Christ fucking shit. Fuck fuck fuck fuck.

What the fuck. Now I'm going in there to sort it out with them. Figure out real nice why they thought they could ever do anything without me. Figure out why they thought they could do anything without me starting it. That's not fucking allowed even a little bit.

I bounce in and then I stand right in front of that fucking not nice mother fucker. Did you fucking leave me out of something? He doesn't respond, and I say I don't need an answer. You think? He says, can you believe this shit, I don't know. I don't know? That's not fucking allowed.

At this point, I fucking slap the mother fucker across the face, but with my fist. As while he's lying on his side, I kick him as many times as I fucking want. Until I am pretty sure I notice he is not moving. I do always know that line. Between life and death. There is quite a bit of playing with him left. He didn't die did he?

I don't think he had. He's barely breathing. I don't see it. I assume he is. Now I go over to the other one. She isn't so scared. Just shaking a little. Gonna take all the violence for her lover. Well alright. And I don't ask her if she knew when she done wrong. I just start fucking wailin' her. Just fuckin hittin' and kickin' her as hard as I fuckin' can.

Then she's rolled over on her side. That's the last thing I want. This one dyin' before I've had a good chance to play with it. No no one wants that in the least.

But I honestly hadn't thought about it, whether I would go too far with this one as well. Maybe I had. She's not movin' either. But surely she's breathin'. She's breathin. I've been lookin' forward to playin' with this one for four years. But they've died before. When I think about things, they do maybe die based on what I've planned. I do know that. So I leave it alone. And I return my fuckin' watch room, and I jack over and over to the look of them being there like dead.

4

I remember the first Dead Bod I ate.

There was something incredibly not wrong with me, I knew that.

It was a female. It was twenty. It was time for it to die.

It was time right that second. I could see the readiness for death. It was the wrinkles around the mouth. It was the slight bags around the eyes, worse than dark cells.

So I fucking killed it.

Then I ate every fucking bit of it. Even the bones.

*

One

--

And what the fucking fuck did you think was
happening? Now they are lying there, holdin' each
other, approximately as dead as it is possible to
fuckin' be. Oh my god it's so hot. She like strokes his
hand, and it's like it used so much of her energy,
she's way closer to death after. They're nearly dead,
and they want to make porn. Oh my god, I'm jackin'
so hard I can't feel my dick, and I'm trying hard to find
the feelin' again. It's gonna be so epic I can wait a

second, in fact, I'm laughin' my head off.

The two them are thinkin' they're gonna kiss. I can tell. They're holdin' each other around the necks at this point. And I allowin' because this is a hot jack. Maybe they're waitin' to come back around a bit. Waitin' to feel they ain't dying no more. Then there gonna go for it. Wait. Here we go. They're going for it in death. They're going to die fucking.

She's climbin' on top of the fucker. This one is always getting' her cum on. Oh my god, she's struggling to lift herself. Oh so much pain, her arms are so hurt, wah wah wah. Oh she's up! And she's like making love to him. Ha ha ha ha. Oh I want to feel something here!

But I'm not feeling anything. It does feel any good. And I'm fuckin' needin' to feel something. Right this fuckin' second.

I get up and stand right in front of the peer-through wall. And I jack as mightily as I can. I'm going, and I'm going, and I'm going.

Can I do anything more to bring this orgasm to me? No I don't think that I can. Actually there always is. More pressure. And I squeeze with all my might.

And all of the sudden I do feel something. At the base of my dick I get the insane pleasure. A bit of pain, but that's all pleasure to me. Just tons of pleasure, tons of great feeling. And then I am feeling amazing!!!

But then I'm twerking and I realize something is wrong. My dick flies off and up and into the air. And as I'm writing to you I think this is the end of my story. I wrote I need to fuckin' tell you in 45 minutes here.

And now I have to go kill them. Because the Dead
Bod Man is Dead. And everyone else is gonna die.

*

Three, two, one. I need a fucking Dead asshole right

this second. This isn't fucking okay.

This is not fucking okay.

I can't fucking stand a fuckin' second of this.

I need the Dead Flesh. The Dead Hole. Right this

second.

I'm gonna kill em'. I gonna end it right here.

*

Two

--

I am fuckin' ragin'. I mean this is the most poetic
moment of all time. If the Dead Bod Man is gonna die,
I mean, he's gonna kill quite a few people first. Is it
not the case everyone everywhere is gonna die,
maybe it isn't. I can see that. The Dead Man can see
when a thing isn't possible. But he hadn't been
planning it. And it wasn't really something he was

thinking of. The point was to scare literally everyone, so they had needed to be alive. They needed to see and viscerally experience what the Dead Bod Man had done, and they needed to be awed, by what the Dead Bod Man had done.

So I rushed the fuck in there, and I fuckin' ragin'!!!! I'm ragin' mad!!!! She's on top of that mother fucker, and she doesn't stop, like their love is more important.

Hahaha, what the fuck! Basically the best option to get some final satisfaction is just to fucking kick her off him. And then jam my head in her cunt, and then just try to eat her body from the inside.

She flies on to the fucking ground. She's naked, and I pick her up, and I thrust my head right into her cunt. I take a good sniff o'it. A good deep whiff. Then I just start fuckin' chompin' down. Eaten her cunt, eaten her fuckin insides. She'll be dead in minutes.

I have to say I ain't never killed no one this way. I eaten for sure. But this is actually the most erotic thing I ever fuckin' thought of. Then all of the sudden someone is pushing me form the side. The fucker thinks he'll fuckin' fight to keep his broad alive. Hahahahahaha.

He pushes me again, and I stumble a bit with me head in the woman's cunt. And I just scream so fuckin' loud. Damn I am fuckin' pissed!!!!

I scream and then I turn around and I kick at the fucker. I know where the fuck he is and he falls back. I take a few munches, getting back into it. But the fucker runs at me again, and I fall over with my head all in her cunt. What the fucking fuck? Am I going to have to leave out of this cunt for a second? Who the fuck would do that? Make me have to get out of it for even a second? Does someone dare do that to the Dead Bod Man? You know what, I think given the circumstances, I'm going to have to say that he had. And I going right after him. In fact I'll have to pop out of this thing for a second, and go fully get the guy.

So I pop out of it. And I am ragin' harder than I ever have, harder than anyone had ever thought possible. And I am so ready to destroy the guy, I just roar, the loudest roar, like a fucking tiger. And then I charge at the mother fucker, while my roar Is reverberating off the fucking walls and ceiling.

Then I slam the sad fucker down with both my hands, and I kick him and kick him. I kick him specifically in the nuts. I know how to pop one of the fuckers, and I pop one. Then I lean down and I'm beaten with my first. Just punching his chest, punching his face.

I hear some noise, and I know that fucker is getting up to get away. I just know it. It's a little farther away. You can't fucking trick me!!! But I'm ragin, and I just keep punching, and I just keep fucking beatin' him up.

Then all of the sudden, some fucker has shot me. I hear the gun shot, and it's through my back. I could live through fuckin' anything so I just keep punchin' Holden. Then, one goes through my fuckin' skull. And I think I'm ko'd. Fuck. I'm losing touch a little. My eyes are closing. My heart doesn't want to beat anymore. My world is ending. And that's it.
Bye!!

5

One

-

In the next few hours after the Dead Bod's Man bittersweet death, Holden held Fionae at first while she balled, whilst his nut hung out of its socket, and blood poured from there, from his chest, and from his face.

Fionae had been clinging to life. After NYPD Detective Bernardo Soulaz had shot the Dead Bod Man, paramedics on scene were called down into the bunker, and they immediately noticed a volcano like leakage of blood from her vaginal area. He had chewn significant chunks into it, taken small chunks out of a few organs.

Holden was worried about her, but there was nothing

to do until medical help arrived. He hadn't really noticed as Fionae became faint, and started to pass out. And she fell to the ground just as the paramedics arrived. While not having much strength, Holden caught her with one of the paramedics, and prevented her fall.

From that moment, she was unconscious, and she was taken to the ambulance for care. Once they were relatively certain she would survive, they rushed off with her in the back. The transport to New York-Presbyterian hospital would take thirty minutes, while they sped around congested traffic on the freeway.

Holden was left there, sad and unsure, once again, what would be the fate of his true love Fionae.

6

One

-

The extent of Fionae's injuries was massive. In terms of bleeding, they could not remember having had someone lose so much blood three transfusions later, she was stable. There were also three surgeries to repair internal organs, and to repair the structure of her vaginal tract.

She remained in the hospital two months. She emerged sore, still healing, though expected to fully recover from a cannibalistic attack by the Dead Bod Man. She would never leave the scars from his menacing violence behind; they would remain with her until she died.

Across tv stations throughout the world, the Dead

Bod Man could be seen lying dead in his bunker. He could then be seen carried out under a tarp, and driven away by crime scene specialists.

Exposes traversed through the bunker, explaining the uses of some of the torture devices and areas in the bunker, and estimating the uses of other devices, and areas.

Family members of lost ones were informed of the tragic news that it had been the Dead Bod Man who had taken the person's life. They exploded in to tears whilst the nation watched, and really while every nation watched. Sometimes crews interviewed victim's family members in London, or Hong Kong, and they cried while trying to describe their emotion with varying levels of English.

Forever after there was as saying, that was like being fucked by the Dead Bod man, and the thought sent shivers down the back of every individual that ever said it, or heard it said.

Two

-

From the moment Fionae returned home from New York-Presbyterian hospital, she had wanted to make love to her husband. They were married the first day she came out of the hospital, feeling more emotionally close than ever.

They consummated their marriage in their new penthouse apartment in a brand-new building above

Park Avenue, a wedding gift for their assistance in ending the reign of the supposed worst serial killer in human history. Beneath a glass canopy in the master bedroom, they fucked all night long, even though their stitches brimmed on breaking, and on occasion a few had obviously given way.

And that was a substantial part of their life, until they had given birth to children, and spend most of the day being parents. Though they still continued to cherish sexual pleasure while their kids were at school, and in the night. Sometimes it was like nothing changed at all, with Holden working at home, with Fionae taking time off. And when they were old, and their kids were gone, and they seemed tired, nothing had changed, and they still expressed themselves with sex, and still more than met their needs with each other.

*

Enveloped in the cold, no good to be buried.

Burned like hermits in a house fire,

Thrust into the air, and gone forever.

In the soil, perhaps, in the water, perhaps.

That encapsulated evil, to rise again, in time,

After many years, when you won't expect it again.

*

Each day and each night we're driven to find,

And vanquish our appetites.

In terms of the sexual appetites, they to some seem

to stretch to wherever there is no space, no time.

Otherwise, it leaks out, the same cellular process,

Growth, expansion, multiplication, reproduction,

In a dick suck, in an anal fuck, in a menage-a-trois.

In a wad of cum, launched and packaged in the side

of the mouth,

Of a sex worker.

*

Who was the Dead Bod Man?

What was his name?

Did he go to high school?

Did he ever have a normal life?

He was dangerous from the beginning, he preferred being alone, until he struck.

But if you hadn't known him, he seemed normal, and until halfway through his life, you could mistake him for a normal, patient person. If you hadn't known the backstory. If you hadn't known what his problems were.

In fact, he might have said to you, mid-career, would you like to be, the Dead Bod Man?

*